Jack Sprat Could

by

Sharon Ervin

Jack Sprat Could

Cover Art by *Kristian Norris*

The Wild Rose Press, Inc.
PO Box 708
Adams Basin, NY 14410-0708
Visit us at www.thewildrosepress.com

Publishing History
First Mainstream Mystery Edition, 2017
Print ISBN 978-1-5092-1591-1
Digital ISBN 978-1-5092-1592-8

Published in the United States of America

"She didn't even recognize you.
Does that bother you?"

"What are you asking, Wheeler? Do you think I should feel like a has-been?"

Gray winced. "You know perfectly well that wasn't what I meant."

MaryBeth wasn't in a mood for placating. "Yes, well, maybe I do feel a little over the crest of my modeling career, but then looking at you makes me feel better." She gave him a sidelong glance and he braced himself. "I am consoled by the thought that it's better to be a has-been than a never-was."

Gray said a quiet, "Touché." At the same time, he made a mental note. Crossing verbal swords with MaryBeth Gilland could be hazardous to one's ego, although the damage was mitigated by the sparkle in her eyes and the hint of a smile just before she zinged him. This partnership was working out fine, just fine.

Acknowledgments

I want to thank Ronda Talley and Jane Bryant
for seeing flaws in the galley proofs
that were invisible to me;
and
Editor Laura Kelly for her insights, prodding,
and the occasional psychological boost.

Dedication

To Bill,
who always gets us where I want to go.

Old English Nursery Rhyme

Jack Sprat
Could eat no fat,
His wife could eat no lean;
And so,
Betwixt them both,
They licked the platter clean.

(from *The Real Mother Goose*,
published 1916 by Rand McNally)

Chapter One
Interviews

He saw her through the glass wall of the office, did a stutter step, and stopped. Gray Wheeler recognized MaryBeth Gilland in a heartbeat, standing at the receptionist's desk in his own office.

Pictures did not do the woman justice, not the color spreads of her modeling in charity style shows, newspaper mug shots, or television footage covering her many social activities.

Wheeler swelled to his full six feet, squared his shoulders, buttoned his shirt collar, and secured the knot in his tie. He frowned when he thought of the new worsted silk sport coat tossed over a chair in his private office.

He sucked in his stomach and vaulted through the entrance to "Your Eyes Only Detective Agency, Gray Wheeler, President." The print was gold leaf superimposed over a black painted eyeball.

Ignoring Ms. Yehle's greeting, he cleared his throat to interrupt the receptionist's patter, lowered his voice, and said, "How do you do, Ms. Gilland." He dusted his fingers over the front of his shirt before reaching to shake her hand. "I'm Gray Wheeler."

The former debutante pivoted a quarter turn and focused the legendary green eyes on his face.

Women usually smiled when their eyes met his for

the first time. Gray liked to believe the ladies who claimed they were captivated immediately; who later swore his dark lashes and rugged good looks haunted their daydreams. MaryBeth Gilland obviously hadn't gotten the memo. Instead of giving him the standard appreciative once-over, her expression remained fixed as she floated closer and permitted his larger, calloused hand to envelop her tapered, manicured one.

It took all the self discipline he possessed to quiet the palpitations of his galloping heart, to hold cool and steady his captive hand in her grasp. Giving hers a tug, he said, "Come, let's step into my office."

Without releasing her hand, he yielded the floor, indicating the way to his inner sanctum. Struggling against latent male instinct to somehow stake his claim to this female, he allowed her to remove her hand from his grasp, and he retreated a step. He didn't want to impede her flow as she drifted around him, moving the direction he indicated, toward the door with his name embossed, also in the gold leaf. At that moment, he was glad he had paid extra for the embossed gold. A woman of her discriminating taste would recognize the difference. He wondered if he should call it to her attention, then decided that would be gauche.

He shoved the door wide with one hand, the other at the small of her back, and followed her inside. Afraid he might babble if he spoke, Gray motioned her into one of the leather chairs facing his desk as he casually retrieved the high-dollar blazer from the other one.

Avoiding eye contact, she smiled demurely at the desk and lowered herself to the chair's edge, while Gray backed up to kick the door closed in Ms. Yehle's face, just as the receptionist was drawing breath to natter on.

He ambled around the desk trying to appear cavalier and sat tentatively in his chair. "What can I do for you, Ms. Gilland?"

Face-to-face, he found her even more stunning—long, lithe, fragile. Her skin was golden. Her blonde hair reflected the light of the office fluorescents as her celebrated jade eyes scanned the room.

"I'd like a job."

He wanted to look amenable, not stunned, certainly not eager. He definitely didn't want her thinking he was a sure thing. He paused an extra moment to digest her rather astonishing request. Finally determining that he must not have understood her correctly, Gray folded his arms across his chest, nodded—sagely, he hoped—and concentrated on keeping the excitement out of his voice as he said, "Un-huh."

Her eyes finally ended their appraisal and settled on his face. "I need a job, actually."

"You don't mean need as in need?"

"Yes, I do. Exactly." She nodded, looking at him, or maybe through him. "My family owns this building, your business, maybe even the furniture in this room." She indicated his scarred mahogany desk—the closest thing he had to family—then continued speaking.

"When Dad died...well, there has developed what the lawyers call a 'cash flow problem.' I have a B.A. in history and political science, but I have recently discovered that doesn't qualify me to do anything. The problem is, I need to support myself now, for a while, that is, if I can."

She gave the room another visual sweep and again seemed to avoid looking into his face. "My family's carried you for years." Her eyes cast a quick look at him, then darted away. "In fine fashion, it appears. Everything you have asked, we have provided. I've seen your file, the correspondence. Now one of us needs something from you."

Gray frowned in disbelief, eased back in his chair, swiveled to look out the window, a limited view, the brick wall of the adjacent building.

"What about family friends?" he asked, swiveling back, unwilling to deny himself even a moment of the look and aura of this enchanting woman. He caught her eyes that steadied on his face, then wondered who had caught whose.

"There are possibilities. I can marry." She broke the visual link between them to stare at the floor. "Or I could leach off of one of Daddy's business associates. Some would hire me without saying obvious things. I want something different. Something adventurous."

"Do you know anything about investigations?"

Her hair shimmered as she shook her head. "Only what I've seen in movies and on television."

"It's not a pleasant business. You see the...ah... seedy side of life."

"That's one of those obvious things I mentioned." Her catlike eyes cut to him, suddenly all business. "I've seen your monthly reports. This place has been a charity for the last three years, a tax write-off for a corporation too big to care."

Gray glowered at her for a moment, resenting her verbal assault, but he relaxed as he pondered. What she said was true, of course, and it had not happened by chance. There was a long silence.

"You are gorgeous," he said softly. She remained

silent, as if she hadn't heard. He straightened, pulled his chair up closer to his side of the desk, and propped both forearms on the surface, again wishing he were wearing the jacket that now hung on the coat tree in the corner. He didn't remember having hung it there.

"When business circumstances needed this agency as a write-off," he said, "we complied. When we need to provide the golden egg, we can do that. It's called versatility. Actually, we are already out of the red this month and it's only the..." he stretched his neck forward to check the desk calendar, "...the twenty-seventh."

Her eyes widened. "What does that mean?"

"It means, dear lady, that the rent is paid and the salaries are covered due to sweat and diligence and know-how."

MaryBeth stood, bringing Gray quickly to his feet as well. She had to be five-foot-ten in heels, able to look him almost squarely in the eye.

Her initial timidity was gone.

He continued speaking, bluff and bluster, anything to delay her departure. "It means we stand ready and able to help a lady in distress."

Her eyebrows arched.

"Within reason, of course," he added, making his voice less forceful.

"You will hire me then?"

Wheeler stepped around the desk, then backed against it, bracing himself on one hip to study her as he nodded, hoping his posture and his gestures looked thoughtful and wise.

"On a trial basis, of course." He planned to give ground grudgingly as he maneuvered toward full capitulation. "I'll start you at the standard base salary."

"Oh, no," she cooed, allowing a taunting smile. "You will be gaining the benefit of my name and family connections. I want a percentage of the take."

"What?"

"Let's say ten percent of everything that comes through the door."

Gray pursed his lips, tempted to agree, but checked himself. He didn't want to make it too easy. She was accustomed to easy. So was he. He shook his head, trying to look as if he were contemplating. "Tell you what I could do. I could pay you a percentage of the cases you work on."

She didn't respond, taking her turn to contemplate, so he continued pretending to think aloud. "You'll begin slowly, of course. Work with me. I always take the high-dollar cases myself, anyway."

Slowly she released the dazzle of that famous easy smile. Obviously she felt neither threatened nor intimidated. "Fifty-fifty?"

Oh, he liked that smile. He liked the whole impossible-to-imagine situation. Mostly he liked the schoolboy giddiness in his stomach. He knew it wouldn't last—she wouldn't last—but he would enjoy the moment.

"Eighty-twenty," he haggled, "my way."

She stuck out her hand. He grinned and shook it as she said, "When do I start?"

"Right now, if you want." Again he was slow to relinquish the physical contact of the handshake with her.

"Where do I work?" She withdrew her hand in what was obviously a practiced motion.

"We all have desks."

"Where's mine?" She turned and started toward the door.

"I've got plenty of room. We'll move one in here."

Her smile held. "I wouldn't think of it." Her concern looked feigned as she glanced toward the outer office. "I'd better start out there someplace. We don't want anyone to think there's hanky-panky in the boss's office."

"We don't?" He gave her his best smile and arched his eyebrows.

She matched his best with one of her own. "No."

"Okay you can start out there and slowly work your way in here."

"Then where would you go?"

Was she pretending all that innocence? No, she was toying with him. And he wanted to encourage her to continue doing it.

She said, "I wouldn't consider displacing you...not until I've been here at least six weeks." Her teasing tone reverberated in her smile.

He suddenly went on alert. "Is that a threat?"

"Being out of the red is not the same as showing a profit, Mr. Wheeler. Isn't this supposed to be a profit-making organization?"

Without intending to, he relaxed again as his eyes feasted on her. He liked this whole set up, particularly her. He even liked feeling endangered.

He leaned back across the desk and tapped the intercom. "Ms. Yehle, ask everyone who's available to step into my office."

Gray introduced MaryBeth to the handful of people as they filtered in: wiry Doc Tooker, retired language professor and resident historian; Dorothy Lyng, whose middle-aged mellowing made her a nearly undetectable tail; Dean (Dizzy) Gillespie, who worked crossword puzzles, studied chess moves and, blindfolded, could describe in detail every person in the room, and the diminutive Ms. Yehle, meticulous to the point of being tiresome, yet always, dependably keeping the office on track.

Only the perennial student Tony Jedlicka was missing. Hustling a game somewhere, no doubt.

Wheeler smiled at his staff. "We've got a new mission, people. We are going to make a profit."

They looked alarmed, obviously stunned by his statement.

"The next four days, finishing out the month, are hereby dedicated to making money."

"What do you mean by that, exactly?" asked Ms. Yehle, the only one who had accepted his offer to sit.

"No discounts. No rebates. No more mister nice guy. Every effort we make in the next client's behalf, we compute to money and poke into the corporate coffer. Got that?"

They all nodded soberly, stealing curious glances at the shapely newcomer who appeared to be responsible for the radical change in policy.

"That being the case," Ms. Yehle said, rising, "there's a Treena Flowers waiting to see you."

"Right." Wheeler dismissed the gathering with a wave. He caught MaryBeth's arm and positioned her near the door as the others filed out, muttering polite variations of, "Nice to meet you" and "Glad to have you with us." Then he nodded for Ms. Yehle to send in the client.

Moments later, a breathless Treena Flowers fairly exploded into the room.

Chapter Two
The Case

Treena Flowers was a large woman, expensively dressed. Her hair had a bluish tint and obviously was newly coifed. She was about five-foot-six, Wheeler judged, reeked of perfume, and weighed, conservatively, between two hundred-eighty and three hundred-twenty pounds. A large purse swung from her left shoulder, and her left hand clutched a satchel, an oversized briefcase of some kind.

She lurched to a stop just inside the door.

"Mrs. Flowers?" he said, taking her free right hand, "I'm Gray Wheeler, and this is my…er…my associate, MaryBeth Gilland. Come in and…a…sit down." He had very nearly said take a load off and was glad he had caught himself in time.

Wheezing, Mrs. Flowers filled the chair Wheeler offered. She put down the satchel and pulled the purse into her abundant lap. Gray pointed MaryBeth toward another chair. She moved that way but didn't sit. He followed.

"That's two dollars," he whispered near MaryBeth's ear.

"For offering the woman a chair?"

"Getting the door and the chair. Service is what we sell. You've already made forty cents and the case is not yet afoot."

Pacing to the door, Gray closed it to afford them privacy, then walked back to his desk and perched on the front edge, bracing himself with his hands on either side, flexing and smiling. Didn't hurt to give the ladies a little thrill.

MaryBeth seemed to be studying Ms. Flowers' profile, while Gray studied hers until the older woman caught her breath.

"Now Ms. Flowers," he said, finally forcing his attention to their client, "how can we help you?"

Ms. Flowers pulled a tissue from her purse and dabbed at the rolls of flesh at her neck. "My sister Clover is being murdered."

MaryBeth straightened. "Right this minute?"

"No. Well, yes, she is, too." Flowers continued mopping creases between her abundant chins. "She's in the hospital as we speak. She's had a stroke or something, they say, but Leland is responsible. He has done this evil deed. You can take my word for that."

Gray frowned. Ms. Flowers suddenly had his full attention. "Maybe you'd better start at the beginning, dear lady."

At the words dear lady, MaryBeth shot an accusing look his way. Catching the look, he smiled and shrugged, thankful that Ms. Flowers had missed the exchange.

"To begin," the woman said, shifting her weight and nestling deeper into the chair, which groaned objections with her movements, "Clover has always been naïve about men. Actually, she's always been a little naïve about life.

"You see, we were sheltered as children. She is my older sister, actually, yet I've always had to watch out

11

for her."

Gray interrupted. "How old is your sister, Ms. Flowers?"

"Let's see. I am fifty-one, so she is nearly fifty-four."

"I see. Please go on."

"Clover and I have always been what you might call large-boned. Our parents were both big. It's just in the blood, you know. Of course, it's never caused any health problems, at least not before."

"You and your sister are about the same size, I take it," Gray said, interrupting again.

"Well, no. Actually, I have always been the smaller and, if I can be perfectly candid, the more attractive of the two of us."

Gray nodded, eased off the desk, and strolled over behind MaryBeth to whisper, "These nods are running her a buck apiece. I'm keeping a tab. Okay?"

MaryBeth shrugged as if shooing an annoying insect, and said, "Please continue, Ms. Flowers."

"Clover and I have always used Mr. Younger of Younger and Zale as our lawyer." The client pulled a battery-operated fan from her purse, turned it on, and aimed it directly into her face. "He helps us take care of our business." The fan gave her voice a singsong quality as she raised and lowered her chin. "Clover has a trust fund established by our father years ago. Mr. Younger manages it. Of course, he has always done all our tax work."

She stopped moving and speaking until she seemed satisfied that both Gray and MaryBeth were paying rapt attention. Both nodded, but neither spoke.

"Last spring Leland Sprat worked for their firm

doing tax returns. Leland is an accountant, and a fairly good one, it appears. Anyway, that's where Clover met him, at Younger and Zale."

"Can we assume you met Leland Sprat there, too, Ms. Flowers?" Gray asked.

"Yes, of course, but it wasn't the same." She cut her eyes at him. "Please do call me Treena."

His smile felt plastic. "All right, Treena. Now, what do you mean? Why wasn't your meeting with Mr. Sprat like your sister's?"

"Leland was very curt with me. Very businesslike. Very accountant like."

"But he wasn't 'accountant like' with your sister?"

"That's right. He was charming and overly attentive to her questions. He bowed and scraped her into chairs, and seldom let his eyes leave her, even for a moment."

"How did she react to his attention?" Gray asked.

The woman gave him an impatient look. "How does any woman react to the attentions of an attractive man? Particularly an attractive younger man? Naturally she was flattered. She flushed and giggled a lot. She was quite sophomoric about it. The first thing I knew, she was going out to dinner with the man, and him only thirty-six years old! I really couldn't imagine his motive for initiating a date."

"When was this?"

"The weekend before Easter."

MaryBeth, hands clasped in front of her, stepped forward. "Ms. Flowers, I hate to interrupt, but this murder that you suspect is occurring, is there any urgency?"

The older woman looked surprised. "No, I don't

think so. I think the deed is done."

MaryBeth stepped closer, ignoring Gray, staring intently into Ms. Flowers' face. "You mean you suspect Leland Sprat tried to kill your sister and failed?"

Ms. Flowers returned the intensity. "Oh, no. I think he tried and succeeded. She…ah…she just hasn't quit breathing yet."

Gray tapped MaryBeth's shoulder, and she retreated a step as he said to Ms. Flowers, "Maybe you'd better give us the whole story."

"Well, before I had hardly had a chance to get acquainted with Jack…"

"Jack who?" MaryBeth asked abruptly, interrupting again.

"That's Leland's nickname," Ms. Flowers said, not impatiently. "You know, after the nursery rhyme, 'Jack Sprat could eat no fat, his wife could eat no lean, so, betwixt them both, they licked the platter clean.'"

MaryBeth and Gray both nodded sagely, their puzzled expressions unchanged.

Gray again leaned near MaryBeth's ear. "Do you want me to tally your nods, too, or will you keep track of your own?"

MaryBeth frowned slightly and brushed her hair back with her hand, again as if swiping at an annoying insect. Obviously interested in Ms. Flowers' account, she remained focused on the client.

Wheeler regarded his new associate's concentration and couldn't help smiling.

"Anyway, before I had a chance to have him checked out," Ms. Flowers continued, recapturing the spotlight, "Clover called one afternoon to tell me they were getting married. You could have knocked me over with a feather."

Gray raised his eyebrows at the prospect but swallowed any wayward comment.

"Had your sister been married before?" MaryBeth asked, obviously making a concentrated effort to ignore Gray.

"Great heavens, no. Clover had never even had a…well…a relationship…if you know what I mean."

MaryBeth and Gray nodded solemnly in unison as Mrs. Flowers looked from one to the other.

"My dears, Clover has led a very sheltered life. She had no idea of the er…ah…the rigors, shall we say, of marriage. I tried desperately to talk her out of it. She had only known the man for a few weeks, and we didn't know anything about his background or his marital history or anything. She married him anyway, over my strenuous objections."

Gray folded his arms across his chest. "Ms. Flowers, are you married?"

"Not at the present time, Mr. Wheeler." Brightening, using her hands to push herself up straighter in her chair. She cut her eyes, giving him a winsome look. "Please do call me Treena. Are you…married, that is?"

He cleared his throat at the spark of her possible interest. "No, I'm not. Why don't you continue."

She smiled coquettishly and nodded understanding that made him squirm. "Well, Jack moved into Clover's apartment, which is quite nice. He fooled around, said he was doing tax work out of their home, but he didn't really work, you know. I don't know where he would have come up with any legitimate work to do, unless he was freelancing for Younger and Zale. Anyway, he was there in the house constantly.

"Jack fancies himself a gourmet...a fancy cook, you know." Her chair groaned again as she shifted. "Anyway, he began cooking these very exotic foods, devoting himself to cooking almost all day every day.

"You may recall that I said Clover was always large. Well, I didn't see my sister for a while. Of course we talked every day on the telephone. She confessed she gained eighteen pounds the first week they were married."

Gray whistled and MaryBeth gasped.

"I imagine that may be some kind of a record, don't you think?"

MaryBeth recovered to ask the next question first. "Were they compatible in other ways?"

Ms. Flowers fidgeted, but Gray had the feeling she was excited about getting down to "the juicy stuff" as she continued.

"Without going into a lot of tasteless detail, I will say that Clover told me stories of making mad, passionate love three and four times a day during those first weeks. And her fifty-four years old, for crying out loud."

Gray glanced at MaryBeth, sucking in his cheeks to combat a smile, while his new associate looked from Ms. Flowers to the pattern on the carpet, biting her lips and avoiding his eyes.

"My word," she whispered.

"That's not how you think he's murdering her, is it?" Gray asked.

"Of course not. She was absolutely ecstatic about that part of it."

"But you didn't see her for a while, is that right?"

MaryBeth said, as if eager to move ahead to less sensitive material.

Ms. Flowers pivoted as much as possible in her chair to focus on MaryBeth. "What would you have done? I was afraid to drop by, afraid they might be busy, if you know what I mean. I did telephone. Every evening."

"Did she seem happy?" MaryBeth asked, prodding and repositioning to make herself more accessible to their client's visual path.

"So happy she was silly. She babbled on about S-E-X and used a lot of vulgar terms and suggestive language she had never used before."

"Other than that, did she seem to like being married?"

"Well, other than that, I suppose she sounded like her cheery old self." Ms. Flowers' voice dropped. "When they had been married nearly a month, Clover called and invited me over for dinner. I looked forward to it all that week.

"When she opened the apartment door that night, I was astonished. She looked like the Goodyear blimp swollen for takeoff.

"I said, 'Darling, you are huge!' Jack put his arm around her shoulders, as far as he could reach, kissed her cheek, and said there was just that much more of her to love. Clover's blush practically lit up the room. Can you imagine?"

"Was Leland...er...Jack bigger too?" MaryBeth asked.

Gray gave her an encouraging look, marveling that she had asked such an astute question.

"No," Ms. Flowers said as she, too, gave MaryBeth

an appreciative look, "and that was very strange. He seemed trimmer, more muscular. Later, they showed me why.

"He had turned a spare bedroom into a gymnasium, with all sorts of exercise equipment and machines and gizmos. They said the gym was off limits to Clover. He didn't want her to strain anything."

Gray leaned closer, studying their client's expression, his interest piqued. "Did she object to the gym?"

"Great heavens, no. I gathered that he put it in with her blessings and probably her money.

"The silly thing giggled and rubbed against him like a great, indulged cat. Her behavior during the entire evening was positively nauseating."

MaryBeth eased a step closer. "Were there other changes in her or in her lifestyle?"

"Yes," the woman nodded, flashing MaryBeth another appreciative glance. "They had bought a two-door Mercedes. Can you imagine, a woman her age and size zipping about town in a tiny, little, overpriced sports car. I'm sure she looked as if she were wearing it; as if she had squeezed herself into some ridiculous little red body shaper. How could a grown woman allow herself to be so foolish?"

"Did you stay and have dinner with them that night?" Gray asked.

"Of course. Jack had cooked the whole thing. We had pork roast, yams, creamed pearl onions, homemade yeast rolls, and chocolate pecan pie with a dollop of whipped cream.

"Jack sat at the head of the table and served the plates just like our daddy always did. The difference was that Daddy always trimmed the fat from the meat when he carved. Daddy knew, even then, about the devastating effects of cholesterol.

"Jack served Clover a huge portion of meat, generously rimmed with so much fat that I commented on it, told her she didn't need all that.

"Jack answered with great authority. He said Clover thought the fat contained most of the real flavor of the meat. He said she liked it served that way, and if that's the way she liked it, that's the way she would have it.

"I noticed he trimmed every morsel of fat from his cut. When he caught me studying him, he muttered something about fat upsetting his stomach. Later on, Clover ate those trimmings off his plate for him.

"After dinner, Clover excused herself for a moment. I asked Jack why he encouraged her to eat so much. He said she liked to eat, and he liked to cook. He said he wanted her to have what she liked. I said, 'even if it kills her?' He said she was in perfectly good health. I reminded him she wasn't a young woman anymore. Unfortunately I said that just as Clover came back into the room. She gave me an absolutely murderous look.

"Under normal circumstances, Clover is a wonderfully docile person, seldom gets angry with anyone but most particularly not with me. I was surprised she took such offense at my innocent little observation. She looked like I'd struck her. She didn't talk much after that. I left early."

"Did you see her more often after that?" Gray asked, easing around and backing against the front of the desk again, loosening his tie and letting his gaze shift back and forth between his two companions.

"No." Ms. Flowers lowered her voice and her eyes, again frowning. "After that night, I called them a couple of times a week but they didn't invite me back and I couldn't get Clover to visit me or have lunch or anything. I knew she was getting bigger, though, because of little things she said."

"For instance?" he asked.

"She had to have her wedding ring sized and links added to the bracelet of her wristwatch; you know, made larger."

"I see. Anything else?"

"Yes. She had to keep adding to her wardrobe. Buying larger size clothing." She hesitated. "Anyway, I guess it was six weeks before I saw them again. I ran into them, quite by accident, at a benefit concert Sunday before last. Clover was in a wheelchair. I almost didn't recognize her. My own sister. She was enormous. Her eyes bulged, and her joints—her elbows and knees—scarcely bent at all. Jack was pushing her along talking pleasantly, as merry as you please.

"I said, 'Honey, we need to get you to a doctor.' She said she felt fine. She said she didn't really need the wheelchair, but Jack didn't want her to overexert.

"I was so alarmed, I called Clover's doctor first thing Monday. He hadn't seen her in months. I asked him to drop in on her. He just laughed. He suggested I find a boyfriend of my own and leave poor Clover alone.

"I was so frantic that I called the police. I talked to a Lieutenant Butz."

"Pepper Butz." Gray knew the man. A veteran cop. One he respected. "What did the lieutenant say?"

"He asked me what crime I thought was being

perpetrated." She wheezed and began wringing the tissue with both hands. Her voice rose to falsetto. "I told him I thought my brother-in-law was murdering my sister by feeding her to death."

"What did he say to that?" Gray could only imagine the jokes spawned as word of that accusation spread through the precinct.

"He laughed as jolly as you please. He said if Jack was starving her or beating or injuring her, or mistreating her in some way, the police might be able to intervene, but he didn't know of any law against overindulging someone."

With that, Ms. Flowers jammed the frayed and waded tissue against her nose and began weeping, her massive frame shaking her chair, which creaked and groaned beneath her.

MaryBeth glanced at Gray who returned her perplexed look. Ms. Flowers sniffed, mopped her eyes and nose with the tissue, but didn't look up.

"This morning early," she continued, her voice again higher, "Jack called me. I could barely understand him. He said Clover had had a...a...stroke or something during the night. They were at the emergency room at Mercy." With that, she looked at Gray. "Naturally, I leaped into my clothes and raced right over there."

He nodded solemnly, again fighting the mental picture. "Of course you did. And?"

Flowers dabbed at her nose and struggled with her grief, apparently trying to regain her composure. "The doctor in the emergency room was a Dr. Tate. He was terribly blunt, which is good, I suppose. He said it would be unkind to tell me Clover was going to be all right because she probably was not. He said her physical condition was appalling, but that the really critical factor was her broken leg."

"Broken leg?" MaryBeth repeated, and Gray realized she hadn't spoken in several minutes. She was still standing. He supposed she would sit if she were uncomfortable.

"I was surprised too," Flowers continued, again obviously pleased by MaryBeth's response. "He explained that Clover's morbid obesity had, well, clogged her arteries and that…" Flowers broke down and again began to weep.

Gray leaned forward from his perch on the front of his desk and patted her shoulder.

After a delay, she seemed to regain control. "He said she probably would have been all right, despite her extreme condition, except for the broken leg. He told us that fatty emboli are in bone marrow. I had no idea. He said when a bone is broken, emboli is released; that emboli is just traveling around there in her veins looking for a place to build a dam, so to speak."

With that, Ms. Flowers snatched a new tissue from her purse, covered her face, and began shaking and sobbing all over again. This time she didn't respond to Gray's patting. Gray and MaryBeth held their positions, waiting.

She squeaked the next words. "Dr. Tate said it was just a matter of time until one of the emboli's little dams blocks an artery and…and it…and it kills her." Her voice trailed off in sobs.

Chapter Three
Details

MaryBeth stepped closer but didn't touch Ms. Flowers.

"Did you see her?" she asked, when the crying again subsided. "At the hospital this morning, I mean. Were you able to talk to your sister at all?"

Ms. Flowers blew her nose into the tissue but didn't look up. "I saw her, yes. It was ghastly. She looked pale and huge lying on that tiny slab of a bed in the emergency room, as if she were asleep.

"I touched her forehead. She was clammy. I spoke to her and her eyelids sort of fluttered, but then she began squirming and getting agitated. I didn't want to cause her anxiety, so I left. I ran into Jack who was standing at the admitting desk. He was telling them to do everything humanly possible to save her."

"Did that make you feel more kindly toward him?" MaryBeth asked.

Ms. Flowers regarded the floor as if giving her answer extra consideration. "It sounded good." She raised her eyes to MaryBeth's face. "His inflections were convincing enough and he slouched like he was feeling sorry about things, but his eyes glittered like he was excited. The man is perverse."

Gray stood and rubbed his hands together. "Of course, he might have been revved up by all the excitement and getting her to the hospital." He paused. "How did he get her to the hospital?"

"I don't know."

"You don't know if he called an ambulance?"

"I didn't ask, and no one mentioned how they arrived."

"Do you know what time your sister became ill?"

"No."

Gray paced to a sparsely filled bookshelf on the far wall, then turned and addressed the visitor. "What is it you want us to do, Ms. Flowers?"

"I want you to find out if Leland Jack Sprat has murdered my sister."

"I see."

"You don't have to prove it to the police or a jury or anyone. All you have to do is confirm my suspicions for me.

"I will pay you one thousand dollars a day to investigate Clover's situation. If you do find evidence to indicate murder and Sprat is arrested, I will give you a five-thousand-dollar bonus. If he is convicted, I will pay you an additional ten thousand dollars."

Neither Gray nor MaryBeth spoke.

Apparently recovered and suddenly efficient, Ms. Flowers snapped off her portable fan, stuffed it into her purse, and began gathering her belongings. "Will you people take the job?"

MaryBeth nodded and looked inquiringly toward Gray. He smiled his approval, raised his eyebrows, and nodded back. "You say she's at Mercy Hospital?"

"Yes. Room eight-seventeen. I checked on her just before I came over here."

"Has she wakened?" MaryBeth asked.

"No, she's still unconscious. When I went into her room and spoke that last time, she moved, but she didn't open her eyes. To tell you the truth, I think he has set her mind against me. I can tell you one thing: I intend to make sure Leland Jack Sprat doesn't get away with this."

Ms. Flowers' corpulent hand burrowed deep into the purse and produced a business card.

"I will be either at my home or at the hospital with Clover. Here's my home phone number and my cell. You'll have to look up the hospital's number. I want progress reports."

Using both arms and taking a deep breath, Ms. Flowers hoisted her body up, then bent over to retrieve the briefcase, steadying herself with the arm of the chair. Gray and MaryBeth flanked her as she walked to the door, through the reception room, and out. Then she was gone.

"Where do we begin?" MaryBeth asked, rubbing her hands together, her eyes rounded and shining with excitement.

Gray stifled a smile. "Mr. Sprat sounds like a clever fellow." He basked for the moment in MaryBeth's obvious agreement and regard. "We probably need to find out more about him: where he comes from, police record, everything. And we need to talk to the emergency room people who were on duty this morning, find out how Mrs. Sprat arrived there. However, while he's occupied at the hospital, we might take a peek at the Sprats' home.

"Shall we go at this together or separately?" Her voice rose a third and quaked.

"Together." He arched an eyebrow and gave her

one of his wench-winning smiles.

She seemed not to record any effect. "So we can compare conclusions and get the benefit of each other's observations and theories?"

"Not exactly." He couldn't stop his perpetual grin.

"I'm sure you're right. Let's investigate this thing together."

He grinned broadly. "Good thinking."

Chapter Four
Sprat

"That's odd," Gray mused as he stepped in front of MaryBeth and opened the outside door of the apartment building. He walked through, then held the door for his companion, who followed. A tall man loomed in the hallway, staring at them.

To preempt any questions, Gray said, "Just going up to Sprats'."

The tall man shrugged and bypassed them without a word.

Sidestepping the elevator, MaryBeth hurried up the stairs to the second floor, then turned. "Wouldn't it be smarter to confirm Leland Sprat's exact whereabouts before we go skulking around his apartment?"

"This is less like skulking and more like breaking and entering," Gray assured her.

She looked startled.

"Come on, Gilland, where's the thrill of the hunt if you know exactly where the game is?" He double-checked the apartment number and scowled at the doorknob. "Have you got a hairpin or something?"

"Don't be ridiculous. You sound like someone out of an old B-rate movie." She scrutinized him in disbelief, then looked enlightened. "In fact, you remind me of a reincarnated gumshoe out of a 1940s film."

"Do you have a nail file?" he prodded, disregarding

her comments.

"Yes, I have." She fumbled in her purse.

He enjoyed an uninterrupted study of her concentrating in the several seconds before she produced a file. She started to hand it to him, then pulled back. "I will have to charge you for the use of this instrument."

Wincing, he reached for the knob.

"Wait! What about fingerprints?"

"There are usually too many on an outside doorknob for them to check. They concentrate on prints on inside knobs."

"Oh." She stepped back to allow him access.

The knob turned under his hand. "Never mind the nail file. We won't need it after all."

He strode inside and slapped his open hands against his trousers, assuring he wouldn't touch anything.

Studying his every move, MaryBeth clamped her hands firmly on her purse.

The entry opened into a large living area crowded with Victorian furniture through which there was barely a footpath.

A dining area and kitchen were visible to their left.

Gray gave them a cursory look before he reversed his path, brushing close to MaryBeth, as he advanced to the hallway off the opposite side of the living room. He glanced into, then passed by several doorways before he located the one he sought.

He entered. MaryBeth followed.

The gym, a room which was sixteen feet square, was elaborately equipped. Pulleys for weights were anchored to reinforced beams along one wall and in the ceiling. Gray studied each piece of equipment, leaning, stooping, and peering, without touching. Finally, he frowned thoughtfully at a wooden baseball bat thrust horizontally through the rungs of the lifting bench. He started to reach for it, then pulled back. MaryBeth saw the bat at the same time and she, too, reached for it. Gray caught her wrist.

"What is it?" she asked. "What's wrong?"

"I don't know," he said quietly, "but my butt feels like a whole anthill's doing the Watusi back there."

"Is that what they call 'gut instinct?'"

"Yeah, only I get ants in the backside instead of butterflies in the belly. If you stay in this business long enough, you'll start to get signals."

MaryBeth rolled her eyes toward the ceiling. "Gee, I hope not."

He looked up at the ceiling, following her gaze. "Actually, it's kind of a turn-on."

MaryBeth flashed him a skeptical look, then continued looking around. "I think in this instance, your derriere may be misinformed. I don't think this case has anything to do with a baseball bat."

"MaryBeth, I know these ants. Don't touch that bat."

"Okay, okay. Let's get on with it. How am I supposed to know what makes you…ah…antsy?"

"I don't know. Maybe, hanging out with me, you'll start developing a little sixth sense about these things on your own."

"Do you really think so?"

"No. I figure you're either born with it or you aren't. You've got all the other important equipment, so it isn't likely you'd have any of the fringe benefits." He gave her his most leering smile. "You know what I mean."

She returned his look, all innocence. "You're not saying that just because I had the fingernail file, are you?"

"That wasn't the 'important equipment' that came to mind." He marveled at her quick, glib give and take. He cut a glance out the window, sobered, and caught her wrist. "Come on, let's boogie out to the hospital and see what we can find out there."

"Are we through here?"

"Yep."

"Didn't you think it was a little strange to find the door open so we could just waltz in? Maybe we should look around for signs of an intruder."

"We'll leave that for Lt. Butz." He nodded, indicating the window. "He's on his way up with a mob of armed cops."

Her eyes rounded. "And he might think he's bagged the intruders if he catches us?"

"Right."

"I see. Right. Boogie it is."

MaryBeth stayed in lock step with Gray's shadow as they wound their way back through the over-furnished living room. She jumped at the shrill sound of the telephone ringing as she passed it. Gray looked back.

Biting her lips, she gave him a pleading look. "I really do think we ought to answer it."

"It'd better be a short conversation."

Nodding, she pulled her sleeve over her hand and picked up the phone. "Hello... Yes it is. She's not available right now, can I take a message?" She paused a moment, listening. "Yes. That's all right. I'm sure she'll understand. Thank you."

As she cradled the phone, Gray grabbed her arm and propelled her out the door, down the hallway, and through the exit into the stairwell, instead of waiting for the elevator.

They clamored down to ground level before they stopped at the stairwell's exit. Gray eased the door open and peered out, then stepped back, tapping his index finger against his lips indicating they should be quiet.

MaryBeth's breathing slowed as she stood unmoving next to him. Her knuckles turned white from clutching her purse so tightly against her.

Several minutes passed before Gray ventured another look.

Wordlessly, he took MaryBeth's hand and led her out.

"We almost bought it that time." He continued holding her hand. She kept pace with him as they walked, stride for stride, toward the car. Slowing, he said, "Was the call important?"

"It was someone from Younger and Zale, Attorneys at law. Mrs. Sprat's codicil is ready."

Almost at the car. Gray stopped to look at her. "What's a codicil?"

"An amendment. Apparently she's changing her will."

"Did they say how she was changing it?"

"No. The woman on the telephone apologized for the delay. She said six weeks was longer than it usually takes to draw a codicil but more urgent work kept pushing it back. Mrs. Sprat had indicated there was no hurry. The woman said she hoped the delay had not inconvenienced Mrs. Sprat. Why? Do you think the delay might be significant?"

"Well, ye-ah."

He gave her a 'dumb blonde look.' Her eyes rounded, her eyebrows arched, and her mouth thinned to a narrow line. He needed to rethink the look—his, not hers.

"It could be significant enough to be a motive for a murder," he said. "She might have been cutting good old Leland Jack Sprat out."

"Of course!" MaryBeth dropped back but continued following as he began walking again, pacing to the car. Gazing thoughtfully at the car door he opened for her, she said, "But you could also look at it the other way round. If it was a change she initiated six weeks ago, she might have been adding him as a beneficiary, rather than removing him."

The ants marched again, the trampling of their many feet giving Gray a headache as he waited for MaryBeth to settle into the passenger seat.

As he got into the driver's seat, he said, "Let's go to the hospital and see if Clover Sprat has regained consciousness. If she has, we'll ask her some salient questions."

"About her will? Whatever the change is? That could point the direction for our investigation, right?"

"Also, we might inquire about who took batting practice with her shin." He flashed a mischievous grin.

"Oh, yeah, that, too. I guess knowing who did that could simplify things."

"Yeah." He gave her a wink. She smiled sheepishly.

Chapter Five
The Victim

The emergency room doors swung open automatically when Gray and MaryBeth's approach triggered an electric eye. A nurse briskly pushing an empty wheelchair met them.

"Are you ambulatory?" She gave them both a visual once-over, frowning.

Gray pulled MaryBeth into his arms and did a quick Fred Astaire/Ginger Rogers mime, whirling by the nurse. "Quite." He flashed her a flirtatious grin.

MaryBeth, stepping quickly to avoid his feet, shoved him away, straightened her clothing, flushed, and walked to the reception desk. "We're looking for Dr. Tate. Is he still on duty?"

The receiving nurse behind the desk answered crisply. "Yes, he is, but he's sleeping."

"Here?"

"Weekends, we're staffed on rotation. All of our trauma physicians approved for practice here at Mercy alternate the duty. It is customary for them to sleep when they can. He came on duty at four o'clock this morning. He was very busy until ten-thirty or so. This is the first real break he's had."

MaryBeth placed her manicured fingertips on the admissions desk. "Could we please speak with him? It's important." As she waited for a response, she peered down at the patient admission list on a clipboard on the counter.

Gray stepped closer and flashed his boyish grin, the one that often got him favors with females. "It really is important for us to talk to Dr. Tate."

The nurse's scowl softened, along with her tone of voice, as she turned her attention on him. "I'm really not supposed to, unless it's an emergency, of course. Would you say your business constitutes an emergency?"

Gray's grin became a doleful smile. "It's about a murder in progress. I think that qualifies, don't you?"

As the nurse studied him, her countenance lifted to a look of surrender.

Having finished her study of the patient list, MaryBeth interrupted what may have looked a little like foreplay. "Do you remember Mrs. Sprat? She came in this morning. Had had a stroke or something."

The nurse nodded, without shifting her gaze from Gray's face. "Certainly." Then, as if she were startled out of her reverie, she cast a riveting look at MaryBeth. "She was the large woman with the very…you might say…attentive, very attractive, young husband."

MaryBeth settled a questioning look on Gray, as if mutely asking his permission to continue her questions. He nodded approval and she pressed on. "That's right. We need to see the doctor who treated her. Was that Dr. Tate?"

The nurse frowned another minute, obviously trying to reach a decision. "You will have to take responsibility."

Gray smiled, pleased with MaryBeth's effort. "Fine. We will. We do. Now, where is he?"

Standing, stepping around the counter and turning on her heel without venturing another look into Gray's eyes, the nurse paced briskly down a corridor. Gray and MaryBeth followed.

The nurse stopped in front of a door and rapped softly, hesitated, looked at MaryBeth once more, and entered the room, fanning a hand at them, indicating they should wait. In a minute, she reappeared, threw the door wide, and motioned them inside.

A rangy young man dressed in surgical greens bent over a lavatory splashing water on his face. Turning, he began wiping his face with a paper towel from the dispenser.

He hesitated a moment when he saw his visitors, looking first at MaryBeth, then at Gray, then arching his brows as he directed his attention back to MaryBeth. Inhaling, straightening to his full height, he gave her a provocative half-smile.

"Anthony Tate," he said, offering his hand first to MaryBeth then, releasing his grip slowly, to Gray, but he spoke to her. "You want an update on Mrs. Sprat's condition?"

She gave him a slow smile which seemed to draw him closer a step. "Yes," she said softly. "Everything."

Gray watched with a scowl as MaryBeth blatantly manipulated the doctor with some primitive form of body language, lingo, he realized, with which all three people present in the room seemed conversant.

Tate suddenly looked sincerely concerned. "Are you relatives?"

MaryBeth looked straight into his eyes, as if they were the only two people present. "No, we're not."

"What is your connection?"

Gray cleared his throat, not enjoying his role as invisible mute. "You might say we're employees of hers. Her condition relates directly to our employment. She's had a stroke, is that right?"

Dr. Tate, still concentrating his gaze on MaryBeth, nodded. "Right."

Shuffling his feet restlessly, hoping to demonstrate his angst and draw some of the raw sexual attention drifting between his two companions, Gray spoke again. "Was there anything unusual about the circumstances, anything you might have noticed in your treatment of her?"

The doctor shrugged, as if he found the questions annoying, an interruption of his ogling and whatever thoughts he might be entertaining. "What do you mean?"

"Was there anything odd? Anything that piqued your curiosity?"

Tate's brows furrowed slightly as he turned his eyes and his attention to Gray. "Funny you should ask. There was one peculiar thing."

"What was that?"

"They were so late."

"Do you mean late in the night?"

"No. Her condition. There obviously was some significant delay getting her to the hospital after the initial episode."

"Did you ask about the delay?"

"Yes. I asked her husband. The patient herself arrived comatose."

"She was unconscious? Unable to communicate with you at all?" MaryBeth blurted, drawing looks from both men.

"Yes. Still is." Tate frowned her way thoughtfully.

"You were never able to speak with her, even in the emergency room?"

"That is correct."

Gray studied MaryBeth a moment before he asked the follow-up question. "What did her husband say about not bringing her in as soon as it happened?"

"He said he didn't know she was ill at first. When he finally decided she needed medical attention, he had difficulty transporting her."

"Could that delay end up causing her death?"

"The delay itself wouldn't have been that bad," the doctor said slowly, "if it hadn't been for her broken leg."

"Yeah, what about that?"

"It's her right tibia—her shinbone."

"Now you've lost me, doc."

Tate ran a hand over his head, smoothing his hair, as if trying to stimulate his memory.

"In addition to her stroke, Mrs. Sprat had a broken leg, which really is the life-threatening factor here."

MaryBeth spoke up. "Would you explain that?"

The doctor looked at her as if he were eager to do anything she asked. "As I told Mr. Sprat and Mrs. Sprat's sister earlier, in a normal person, a broken tibia, or any broken bone, for that matter, is not beneficial, of course, but in someone like Mrs. Sprat, someone so morbidly obese, fatty emboli are stored up in the bone marrow. A broken bone releases those emboli into a person's vascular system. We will watch her closely and do everything we can, but circumstances like this make for a combination that is almost always terminal."

"Then you think someone has intentionally

attempted to murder her?"

"Well, no, I wouldn't go so far as to say that." He alternated looks from MaryBeth's hopeful stare to Gray's frown. "I mean, it would be a very inefficient way to do away with someone intentionally." He paused, again, frowning and staring as if searching his thoughts. "Of course, in her case, her general health coupled with the coincidental break, well, the combination of those factors puts her in extremely critical circumstances."

"How was her leg broken, Dr. Tate?" MaryBeth asked. "Could medics have done it loading her into the ambulance?"

He shrugged. "I doubt it. If they had done it, they probably would have mentioned it." His scowl deepened again.

"What?"

"I don't think she arrived by ambulance. I believe she came by private car."

"Maybe her husband injured the leg accidentally, wrestling her around, loading her into his car," Gray said, maneuvering for more information.

"There were no other bruises or contusions. Just this one broken bone. It's a clean break at that. The husband didn't mention anything about it to the admitting nurse. He may not even have known about it. A woman as sedentary as Mrs. Sprat... Well, you just don't expect her to receive a blow like that."

Flashing MaryBeth a significant look, Gray scrubbed his backside against the counter. "A blow like what?"

MaryBeth moved nearer to the sterile cabinets, shifting restlessly, as if she were entertaining ants of her own, but she didn't interrupt as Tate continued speaking.

"The patient's nightclothes were sliding around and one of the nurses saw the fresh bruise on the woman's shin. She called it to my attention, which is how I happened to see it at all. It was obvious that Mrs. Sprat had received a severe blow to the tibia a short time before she was brought in here."

Gray glanced at MaryBeth. Their gazes held as he folded his arms over his chest and scrubbed his derriere back and forth against the cabinet behind him.

She nodded and brushed a hand across her own tush.

He flashed a teasing grin and whispered, "It could be love."

She blinked once, rolled her eyes and dismissed him.

Gray raised his voice to normal volume. "Doc, do you think this mishap could be part of a plan? Is there any way these circumstances could add up to premeditated homicide?"

Tate shook his head slowly. "That is a really far-fetched theory, sir. If you want to murder someone, there are more efficient ways to go about it."

"Do you mean because this way she might not die?" MaryBeth chimed in, again drawing looks from both men.

Tate's perpetual frown deepened. "Given the condition of the victim, in this instance, her death is not all that uncertain."

Gray eased a step forward, studying Tate like a bloodhound on scent. "If he'd gotten a gun and blasted her, it might have been quicker, but it also would have made everyone suspicious. People would automatically suspect foul play." Gray paused, giving Tate time to put things in perspective. "Have you even thought about calling the police, reporting this as a possible homicide attempt?"

MaryBeth's eyes darted between the men's faces. "Did it even cross your mind that her impending death might be the result of a criminal act?"

He looked surprised and confused. "Well, no. There weren't any signs of abuse or past mistreatment." He grabbed his wadded paper towel and used it to wipe drops around the sink where he had splashed while washing his face. "Except for the one bruise, there's no evidence of trauma of any kind. In fact, I'd say the woman appears to have overindulged herself into astonishingly bad health. According to her own sister, she's been using a wheelchair so she wouldn't have the strain of walking."

MaryBeth's growing excitement made her voice warble. "I believe the wheelchair was her husband's idea."

Gray wondered aloud. "Doc, how do you suppose she broke her leg riding in a wheelchair?"

"Wheeler," MaryBeth's tone was accusing, "there would be no way to maneuver a wheelchair through that apartment. She must have walked when they were at home."

"Right."

Tate obviously had become interested. "It's definitely puzzling. She must have been on her feet and run into something—hard."

Gray fumed. "Doesn't look to me like she's been doing a lot of running to have run into anything, hard or not."

Tate nodded agreement. "To tell you the truth, that break looks more like she got hit with a lead pipe, if the length and shape of the bruise is any indication."

MaryBeth's astonished look probably mirrored his as she and Gray responded in unison. "What?"

"A rounded surface. Something like a pipe," Tate mused, as if mired in his own thoughts.

Gray smiled sardonically. "Or maybe a baseball bat?"

"Could be."

"Good guess, Doc. If she dies without any change in her condition, what will you certify as the cause of death?"

Tate stepped toward the door. "First off, I'm pretty sure she is going to die, probably in the next few hours. You've got me curious. I think I'll go down there and have another look at Mrs. Sprat." He opened the door. "We're doing everything we can, of course, but her condition is, I'm almost certain, going to be too much to overcome." He motioned MaryBeth toward the door. "Before you people showed up, I probably would have listed her death as due to natural causes, the result of an embolism." He coughed a little laugh. "I guess that will be the listed cause even after everything you've said. Natural causes. Very strange."

Trailing the men to the open doorway, MaryBeth said, "How many people know that emboli are released into the blood stream from broken bones? That's news to me."

Gray brightened and stopped walking. There was another good question from this rookie assistant.

Tate shrugged. "Anyone with medical training. A

doctor, a nurse, a therapist. Emergency medical techs. It's certainly no secret." Tate stepped up and placed his body against the open door, holding it open for them. "Do you want to come with me while I check Mrs. Sprat?"

"Thanks, Doc," Gray said, taking MaryBeth's elbow and guiding her through the open door, steering her well clear of Tate's body. He recognized the doctor's tactic. It was one he used occasionally, when he wanted a cheap thrill, forcing a woman close in a doorway to enjoy the brush of her body, and the fragrance of her close up.

Tate glowered at him, prompting Gray to offer the medic a knowing smirk as he continued talking. "I think right now we need to find out a little more about Leland Jack Sprat."

With that, he nudged MaryBeth into a quick step down the hall, before he turned.

"One more question, Doc. How can we find out how the Sprats got to the hospital?"

A dozen yards away, Tate said, "I don't know. We were busy this morning. You'll have to talk to whoever worked the door. Does it matter?"

"I don't know, but it's a loose end and those always attract my attention, if you know what I mean." Gray turned to follow MaryBeth, who was nearing the outside door. He admired the view as her hips swished from side to side ahead of him.

On impulse, he glanced back. Tate, too, was standing mesmerized, watching her walk away. The men arched their eyebrows and exchanged knowing looks.

Chapter Six
Morgue

His right hand propped at the small of her back, Gray guided MaryBeth through the lobby of the newspaper building onto the elevator and pushed the selector.

She tossed him a chastising look as his hand maintained contact with her back.

Clearing his throat, he sidled back, rolled his eyes toward the ceiling and whistled a soft tune under his breath.

Seven stories up, the doors opened into a dimly lit hallway. Gray stepped across the corridor and opened the door directly in front of them marked, "Library."

Inside, long, cluttered metal tables welcomed the visitors, mute outposts before a sprawling rank and file of filing cabinets.

Sunlight filtering through dirty windows along the west wall illuminated dust motes hovering above cluttered furnishings and muted the light from ancient schoolhouse fixtures ten feet overhead. The lines of filing cabinets were covered with dust long settled. Dozens of file folders, open and closed, were strewn over the tables. One table held three microfilm viewers and dozens of scattered microfilm cards. A small computer and printer occupied one end of another table. Bound copies of newspapers lay in disarray on the surfaces of three tables.

When Gray and MaryBeth stopped walking and the echoes of their footsteps ceased, the vast room seemed eerily silent, like a deserted city street after a snowfall.

"Where are we?" she whispered, stepping close to his side.

Gray smiled and kept his voice low. "The morgue. The newspaper morgue. It's sort of a historical library. Every bit of information that's ever been printed in this newspaper is right here, if you can find it."

She gave the room a troubled look. "We might have better luck retrieving stuff from the Titanic."

Gray looked around, standing on tiptoe, then stooped to peer under the tables. "Yep, it's formidable." He continued craning his neck, scanning. "Except for the tour guide, one Larry Simonovsky."

She started, grabbed and fisted the tail of his blazer in one hand when Gray shouted. "Larry! Hey, Lar, where're you at, man?"

Both Gray and MaryBeth pivoted as they heard a rustling beyond the stacks on their right. Moments later, a bespectacled man, slim, stooped, thirtyish, and shabbily dressed, emerged. He frowned when he saw them, but the scowl lifted to a smile of recognition.

"Gray Wheeler, you old bandit." His voice sounded husky, as if it hadn't been used in a while. He gave them a silly grin and approached in a kind of disjointed lope that gobbled up the space and ended only when he stood directly in front of Gray.

The man's rimless eyeglasses slipped down his long nose unhampered. He wiped his hand on the front of his shirt before offering it. His grin broadened. "I wondered if you survived the party. Haven't seen you since." He looked at MaryBeth and added, "U.S. Grant High School, Class of '94."

Without taking his eyes from MaryBeth, the man removed his glasses, straightened to six-foot-two—suddenly taller than Gray—and brushed an unruly shock of hair off of his forehead with his fingers. His demeanor changed from absent-minded-professor to quasi-predatory male. MaryBeth's eyes widened at the transformation.

"Twentieth reunion. Major event," Larry continued, narrowing his eyes, appraising her. "Gray entertained. Held us all spellbound with his wild stories and memorable antics."

Gray cast a cautioning look toward Larry, aware of the predatory change in the recluse's physical carriage.

"MaryBeth Gilland, this is Larry Simonovsky. The man, my dear, is a walking encyclopedia. What Larry doesn't know offhand, he knows where to find, and most of that information is available right here"—he waved a hand encompassing the area—"somewhere in this room.

"Naturally, the newspaper's front office forgot about Larry years ago. He has thus become the Quasimodo of city journalism, stuck here in the tower, the forgotten tender of the bell."

MaryBeth shook the hand Simonovsky offered. "Nice to know you."

"Oh, honey, not nearly as nice as it is for me to know you." He paused, emphasizing his next words, "But grand of you to say so." Larry was slow to release her hand. When he did, it was with obvious effort that he refocused his attention on Gray.

"Why am I doubting this is a social call?" He

waited, giving Wheeler a chance to deny the charge, then proceeded. "What is it you're looking for?"

Gray swaggered in place, doing the little step and move athletes use when they want to impress one another by demonstrating their coordination. "Well, Modo," he began, assured he had the spotlight, "there's a guy, a Leland Sprat, sometimes called Jack. We need to know everything you can tell us about him."

Larry eyes shifted back to MaryBeth. "Checking out a new boyfriend?"

She pursed her lips and shook her head, letting the fluorescent lights play their come-hither number on her hair. "Neither Sprat nor Wheeler."

Larry's eyes roved again until they reached her mouth and stopped. "One 't' or two?"

MaryBeth looked at Gray. Larry slowly shifted his gaze to his former classmate, who opened his hands in a helpless gesture.

"One," MaryBeth supplied, when Gray didn't respond.

Gray shot her an accusing look. "How do you know that?"

"The admissions sheet on the counter at the nurse's station."

Gray lost his flash of intensity and smiled, pleased that she had made yet another contribution to their case.

"I'm teaching her the detecting business." He was looking at MaryBeth but speaking to Larry. "Everything I know."

Ignoring Gray, Larry addressed himself to MaryBeth. "I'm not sure who's teaching who. Let's go punch up the name and see what we get."

He reached for her arm, but Gray abruptly stepped

forward, body blocking the researcher's hand before contact.

Larry glowered at his rival male for a moment as he said, "It might help if you give me a list of civic or business organizations he belongs to, or hobbies, and we can run a few of those."

Concentrating on keeping his body between his two companions, Gray said, "Let's try his name first and see how far that gets us."

Larry dragged a metal chair to a newer vintage computer and turned on the monitor, which featured a nude woman screen saver. He gave MaryBeth a sheepish grin before he sat, typed in some instructions, and stared at the screen, listening to the machine hum. A moment later, he shifted his gaze back to MaryBeth.

"Do you date him?" He spoke as if Gray weren't standing at his elbow, making every effort to block the couple's view of one another.

MaryBeth's expression turned to pained. "No, I don't."

"Glad to hear it."

"Not half as glad as I am to say it."

Before Gray could register an objection, Larry stiffened, sitting straighter in his chair and studying the monitor.

"Let's see what we've got here. We have Sinclair, Sprassy, a Jerome Sprat and...ah...yes, here we have Leland (Jack) Sprat, with one 't,' just as you prescribed, my pet." He leaned to see around Gray and flashed a quick smile at MaryBeth, then turned back to the screen, indicating Gray and MaryBeth should watch over his shoulder.

"Pretty colorful character since 2006. Declared

himself a tennis professional that year and got a job at Winterhaven. Signed on in January. Winterhaven's got great indoor courts. I've played there."

The screen flickered, and he squinted as he ran through a hodgepodge of news stories.

"Here. This news article says he was twenty-six when he had a little fender-bender downtown, in 2007. March. Collided with one Margaret Swenson, fifty-seven. The accident did eight hundred dollars' worth of damage to Sprat's Ford Crown Vic.

"Hmmm. Now this is interesting. The next item says Sprat married the said widow Swenson that fall. October 2007. Seems to have been a banner year for your boy.

"He worked on the United Fund campaign that spring. The story identifies him as a CPA associate with Younger and Zale.

"That's unusual, a tennis pro who is also a CPA. Probably be a good idea to take a closer look at his credentials."

MaryBeth stared at the screen. "He married Margaret Swenson in 2007? Is that what you said?"

"Yeah. Pretty startling, that. He was twenty-seven and she was fifty-seven. More than twice his age. Hmmm. Let's check her out."

He tapped more keys. "Next up is her obituary. She died 4 April 2008."

MaryBeth gasped and stared at the screen as if she were trying to corroborate his finding.

Larry half turned, studied her face, then shrugged. "Well, like I said, he was twenty-seven, in his sexual prime. She was fifty-seven. I don't write this stuff, you know. I just dig it up."

MaryBeth put one hand on his shoulder, leaning, trying to read the screen. "What did she die of?"

Larry shifted, leaned closer to MaryBeth and flashed a simpering grin at Gray, but sobered when he saw how intense she was about her question. "Doesn't say." He again turned his full attention to the screen. "You know how they do obituaries. 'So-and-so died at Mercy following a brief illness.' Survivors include husband, Leland, of the home, and a number of nieces and nephews."

"Can you go back and find her wedding announcement?"

He typed some more. "Here it is. Margaret Dove Swenson married Leland Jack Sprat in a civil ceremony October 29, 2007."

"Was Dove her maiden name?"

"Yeah. Very old, very prominent family around here. Big money types."

"So she had been married before? To a Mr. Swenson?"

Gray cleared his throat, reminding his two companions that he was still there. "Was that Dar Swenson, the fish market guy?"

Both MaryBeth and Larry looked at him as if he'd grown horns.

Larry recovered first. "Right."

"Anything else?"

"We're only on computer up here since 2004. You've got what there is on the machine. Before that, it's microfilm back to 1982 or so. Before that, it's dig, dig, dig. I've got some things indexed, but it'll take me some time and research to find more. Is it important?"

Wheeler glanced at MaryBeth who gave him a nod.

"Not for any additional info on her, but the dig is a definite yes on Sprat."

"Okay. Check with me tomorrow. Sometime after lunch." Larry took another long look at MaryBeth and lowered his voice. "You do understand, I'm not doing this favor for my old friend Gray. I'm doing it strictly for you, MaryBeth Gilland. Most of the time when I do special requests, people feel obligated to me."

She gave Gray a quelling look and smiled at Larry, who smiled back before he sweetened the deal. "I've got a friend in police records. I might access her files, as long as I'm at it, if it's real important...I mean real important to you." With that, he flashed Gray a warning look.

MaryBeth pretended not to notice either the innuendo or the visual exchange. "Great. Let me ask, Larry, would social security records show where Leland Sprat worked before he became a tennis pro/CPA?"

Larry again glanced at Gray who remained mute as their host turned a sly smile on MaryBeth.

"You're really getting into this detective work, aren't you, pretty thing?"

"Let's say I have potential." She smiled, but wasn't distracted from her question. "Would those social security records be available to you?"

"Maybe, but it's a hassle if I get caught. That is high risk hacking."

"Will you try? Can you get away with it, without getting into trouble, I mean?"

"Certainly, if you make the risk worth my while." He paused and stared at her a long moment. "I would be willing to take a chance, sweet face...for you." He waited, but she only smiled. "I could perform even better if some really gorgeous creature brought lunch up here tomorrow. That way I'd have extra time and incentive to work straight through."

MaryBeth leveled another quick look at Gray. He said, "I don't think I'm the 'gorgeous creature' to whom he is referring." He thought he detected a blush as his new associate shrugged and blinked agreement.

"Lunch it is, Larry," she said in a businesslike tone. "I'll be back here at noon tomorrow."

Larry smiled at Gray like the proverbial cat that swallowed the canary. "I'll get busy laying things out—information, that is. See what I can turn on...er...up, that is."

It was a frowning Gray Wheeler who caught MaryBeth's elbow and led her briskly toward the exit.

"Good seeing you, Gray," Larry called, standing and strolling along behind them. "Stop by any time, except tomorrow noon, of course. I have very private...very personal...plans."

Gray grunted, but neglected to thank his friend for his help.

Chapter Seven
Lieutenant Butz

Gray and MaryBeth hurried through the automatic doors into the lobby of hospital emergency. As before, a nurse materialized, pushing a wheelchair.

"Are you ambulatory?"

Neither of them responded. Looking beyond both nurse and chair, they swept past, MaryBeth leading toward the bank of elevators. Suddenly, she stopped.

"What's wrong?" Gray asked, almost plowing into her.

"It's weird, but I have this absolutely dreadful feeling. I'm afraid to see him. You know, afraid to see his face with my own eyes."

Gray grimaced. "Okay. We need as much information as we can get before we go head-to-head with him. We've got to do our homework—groundwork—first, then we'll go for the confrontation." He turned to leave.

"But we have to see him." MaryBeth caught his sleeve. Gray frowned at her hand on his arm and she withdrew it.

"We don't even know for sure that he's here," Gray said.

Her jaw locked, her teeth clenched as her lips tightened over her mouth. At the same time her hands fisted at her sides. "Oh, he's here all right, and I've got the ants to prove it."

Gray allowed a wry smile as he addressed the empty hallway. "Now I've gone and done it. I've turned a perfectly lovely woman into a freak."

"Wheeler, contrary your illusions. I was never perfect."

He chuffed a sarcastic little laugh, but the humor died quickly and he folded his arms across his chest. His frown deepened as he studied her face a long moment before he yielded.

"Okay, you may feel like you have to see him, but I don't. I think it would be smarter for one of us to remain unknown to him. It appears that one is going to be me." She started to object, but he held up a hand in her face. "What if we want to follow him later? We don't want him to recognize the tail."

She was grim, but silent.

"Of course, it'd be hard for you to stay incognito for very long anyway," Gray allowed. "I'll go wait in the coffee shop. You go up to the eighth floor and have your peek, then come back by and grab me when you're through."

She bit her bottom lip and took a deep breath. "Right." Turning on her heel, she scurried to a waiting elevator.

Gray followed direction arrows on the corridor walls to the coffee shop.

A woman in white, polishing apples and placing them in a fruit basket display, interrupted herself long enough to draw the cup of coffee he ordered.

Two groups clustered around tables in the room. One bunch, two women and a young man sat quietly. One of the women looked as if she had been crying.

The other cluster, uniformed and looking like medical students, talked in loud voices arguing the merits of what sounded like two different techniques of tonsil removal.

Mulling his own considerations, Gray chose a corner table. Several minutes elapsed before he leaned precariously to pick up a newspaper spread on the next table. He scanned the headlines, settled on a disaster story, and was engrossed when MaryBeth slipped into the chair across from him. She was ashen and shaking.

"It's worse than I thought." She rubbed her hands together as if trying to warm them.

"What is? Did you see him?" Gray folded the paper and laid it aside.

"Yes."

He pushed his coffee cup toward her. She took a long swallow and pushed it back.

"I've had this creepy feeling all day, every time I heard anyone mention Jack Sprat." She looked at Gray as if she were appealing for something. He remained quiet, listening, watching her. "Wheeler, all my life I have liked men."

She hesitated as if she were waiting for him to say something, so he did. "I think it would be accurate to say that all your life, men probably have liked you, too." He gave her a playful smile, trying to lighten her mood.

She stared at him. "I am serious here. I've had recurring nightmares about a man. I've never known who it was because I've never been able to see his face. In my nightmares. I've only seen him from the neck down."

"Clothed?"

"Yes, clothed."

"And you are about to tell me that Jack Sprat is the man of your nightmares, is that it?"

"Right!" She looked astonished by his guess.

Gray shifted his chair forward, put his elbows on the table and leaned close to her, lowering his voice. "Come on, woman, be serious. Think how that sounds."

"I can't help it. In my nightmares, the man is tall and muscular, very well built."

"In all modesty, I'd say that description fits a lot of us."

"No, no, no." She grabbed his sleeve. "This tall, muscular man in my nightmares has some remarkable characteristics."

"You said the guy in your nightmares was clothed, right?" Gray smirked.

"Wheeler, this is not funny. The man in my nightmares has…" she hesitated, rubbing her palms on her skirt. "He has…short arms and…" Her voice squeaked. "Small hands!"

Gray leaned back in his chair, rolled his shoulders, and gave her an incredulous look.

"MaryBeth, MaryBeth," he spoke in a quiet, controlled tone he would use with a difficult child. "That's not how fairy tales go. It's 'My, Grandma, what big eyes you have,' and 'what big ears you have,' and 'what big teeth you have.' There's nothing frightening about 'what short arms' or 'what little hands you have.' Small is not scary."

"Gray, I am serious and I am seriously frightened." She looked toward the exit and clamped her lips tightly between her teeth. "I have to resign from this case. I cannot work on it any more."

"I didn't expect you to last long, but I really thought you were good for more than a couple of hours. I figured you could at least make it through one day." He waited, but she continued biting her lips and rolling her eyes toward the nearest exit. He lowered his voice. "You're not making sense. You know that, don't you?"

"You don't know what this guy does to me in my nightmares."

"What does he do?"

"I don't know. We never get to that part. I mean I run and run and hide and try not to breathe so he can't find me, but he always does. When he grabs my shoulders from the back, I wake up. I wake up scared to death. Sometimes I'm sobbing. I don't know what he does after he gets me because I never stay asleep long enough to find out, thank goodness. What I'm telling you is: Leland Jack Sprat is that man."

"Then you did see Sprat upstairs just now?"

She nodded.

"Did you talk to him?"

"Are you crazy?"

"Did he see you?"

"Probably not. He came out of Room 817 and stopped at the nurses' station. The nurse said, 'Can I help you with something, Mr. Sprat?' That's how I knew who he was. He wanted to know his wife's latest vital signs. The nurse gave them to him off a chart there at the station. She patted his hand—one of those little hands—and looked like she felt sorry for him."

"Are you sure he didn't see you?"

"I don't know. He turned and sort of looked at me before he went back into the room, but I don't know if he really saw me or if he was just looking at a form he saw out of the corner of his eye."

"Your form is pretty memorable."

"Not to a man who's watching his wife die."

It depends on whether he's watching her die sadly or with anticipation."

"All I know is I can't work on this case any more."

"Does that mean no lunch with Larry Simonovsky tomorrow?"

The question obviously was unexpected. Her expression went from fearful to resolved. "Well, no, it doesn't mean that, necessarily. Simonovsky doesn't scare me."

"Being alone with a stranger in that creepy old library, with only a bunch of books to defend you, and Larry with the lecherous leer doesn't scare you, but a big disinterested guy with little hands does?"

"Right."

"So you can continue working on this case, as long as you don't have any contact with Sprat?"

She turned sideways in her chair, crossed her legs and frowned. "That sounds reasonable. Yes, I guess I could do that."

"Okay." Gray stood. "Let's go find a telephone and find out where Lieutenant Butz is right now. I think he needs to know what we have so far." He gave her a warning look. "We will be omitting all references to short arms and small hands."

MaryBeth started to rise, then gave Gray a new frown as she came to her feet. "He's upstairs."

"Who is?"

"Lieutenant Butz."

"With Sprat?"

"Not with him. Near him. He was sitting in the

waiting room reading a newspaper."

"I didn't know you knew Pepper Butz."

"Well, I've never met him, but I've seen his picture in the newspaper, and I'm pretty sure that's who was sitting there."

"Dr. Tate must have called him in on this after we talked."

MaryBeth nodded. "Maybe. Or maybe he's here on some other case. Or maybe he's here for personal reasons. Maybe he's got a family member or somebody in the hospital."

"Yeah. Maybe. Why don't we find out?"

Chapter Eight
Like Minds

MaryBeth Gilland took a deep breath and squared her shoulders as the elevator door opened into the waiting area of the eighth floor. Gray's fingers in the small of her back nudged her. There was no sign of Sprat among the half-dozen people sitting in the area, so she moved forward.

Gray stepped up beside her and, with his hand flat against her back, prodded her toward the man in worn and wrinkled clothing slouched on a vinyl sofa, the man she had thought was Lieutenant Butz. He squinted into a news magazine and clenched the end of a cold cigar between his teeth.

The couple stopped in front of him and stood for a moment, staring until he glanced up. When he recognized Wheeler, Butz closed the magazine, rolled it up, and with some effort, lifted himself from the couch. Wordlessly, he walked to a door marked Chapel and pushed it open. He didn't step inside but held the door open, indicating Gray and MaryBeth should enter.

Again Gray guided his companion, urging her to lead the trio into the empty, dimly lit room. Butz glanced back at the lobby, then let the door swing closed behind him. Gray and MaryBeth turned and faced the lieutenant.

Butz stood five-foot-nine or ten. He had powerful

shoulders and arms, a swarthy complexion and showed his vintage by wearing his sparse stand of light brown hair in a dated crew cut. His posture and clothing made him indistinguishable, yet when he looked at them, MaryBeth recognized a serious depth to his study. Pepper Butz was not a frivolous man.

"Heard you're showing some interest in the Sprats," Butz began without amenities.

Wheeler said, "MaryBeth Gilland, this is Lieutenant Pepper Butz."

MaryBeth offered her hand, and Butz relinquished what she came to realize was one of his infrequent smiles as he shook it. He focused the smile, however, on her hand. Having thus complied with the rules of etiquette, he released the hand. Butz's expression was all business as he turned his dark, prying eyes on Wheeler.

"What kind of case you working? His tone cautioned against flippancy.

Wheeler cleared his throat and glanced at MaryBeth. "It's a little unusual, Lieutenant." He hesitated, digging for a viable explanation. "A woman came into the office this morning all upset. Said she suspected her sister was being murdered, fed to death. Had kind of a tinny ring to it, and we decided to open up the can of worms and do a little digging."

Gray smiled at his own attempt at humor, but Butz ignored him as the officer locked his hands behind his back, pursed his lips, and glared at the floor.

"Treena Flowers." Butz spoke to the floor. "Came to see me a while back." He glanced at Wheeler. "It's like I told her, if a man abuses his wife, dukes it out, or shoves her around, we can take an interest. If he starves her or his kids, his horse, or his dog, even, we can get involved. But a guy who abuses his wife by cooking three squares a day and rolls her around in a wheelchair to keep her from overexerting, well, it's a little unorthodox, you understand, but there's sure as hell no law against it."

MaryBeth looked from Wheeler to Butz. "Then that's not why you're here?"

Butz glowered at her. "Hell, yes, that's why I'm here. After Flowers stopped by, I got curious. I checked to see if Sprat had been married before. Sure as hell. To a very rich old dame. They got married in 2007. In the fall. She was dead by spring."

"How did she die?" Gray asked.

"Natural causes, of course. It was listed on the death certificate as a cerebral hemorrhage. Signed by a doc here at Mercy. No autopsy. They didn't list her height or weight on the emergency room records, so I had to get a warrant and get it from her own doctor. Turns out, she was a large woman. In 2007, Sprat was twenty-seven years old, according to the wedding information. The lady was closing on sixty and had a history of heart problems.

"Besides Sprat, her only heirs were nieces and nephews. I called one of the nephews who lived in Omaha. He said she had a big estate. She changed her will before she married Sprat. Seems she made him sign a prenuptial agreement. She'd inherited the loot from her dad and thought it right to pass the bulk of it on to her dead brother's kids. There were six of them."

"What about Sprat?" Gray pressed.

"Only got twenty thousand dollars."

"Did he collect on life insurance, too?"

"Could have, I suppose. I didn't check."

MaryBeth folded her hands demurely in front of her, summoning their attention. Regarding her, both men paused to allow her a question.

"What about before 2007?" she asked, filling the anticipatory silence. "Did Mr. Sprat have a police record or anything?"

"I thought of that," Butz said, his face showing a little grudging admiration. "There is no paper trail on Leland Sprat before then. It's peculiar. Looks like 2007 is when he got his social security number, his driver's license, and his first job, as far as we can tell."

"He was a little old to be getting his first social security number or driver's license, wasn't he?" MaryBeth puckered her lips into a thoughtful pout.

"Like I said, he was twenty-seven."

"He must have done something before that. He must have driven a car, worked, voted, bought something on credit, been in the military…something." She ventured a look at Gray. "Isn't that right? Shouldn't there be some record of a man before he was twenty-seven years old?"

Gray didn't answer, and she looked to Butz in time to see his admiring look dissolve to a puzzled frown.

"I had those same questions myself. It's hard to believe the man didn't leave a trail of any kind, but he didn't…any I can find anyway. I even got his fingerprints off of a pop can he threw in a bin." MaryBeth looked hopeful. He shrugged, shaking his head. "Nothing. As you can see, it's not for want of trying."

MaryBeth tapped a manicured fingernail against her bottom lip, again drawing the attention of both of her companions. "He was filling space somewhere. There has to be a way to find out what he was doing and where he was doing it."

Butz slanted her another admiring look and stood a little straighter. "All I can tell you for sure is that he wasn't in the military and didn't have a police record, at least not as Leland Jack Sprat. I faxed inquiries to a bunch of places, checked on possible military service. Nothing. I finally emailed my congressman. His office couldn't turn up anything either. The State Department of Vital Statistics doesn't even have a certificate of birth for the guy."

Gray arched his eyebrows and pointed his index finger at the ceiling. "Now, there's something significant." He said it a little too loudly. "The suspect wasn't born, which means he probably was hatched, or maybe reincarnated. That information should guide our search."

Both MaryBeth and Butz shot him annoyed frowns.

He offered a wilted smile as he looked from one chagrined face to the other. "I was just trying to get into this private conversation."

Butz nodded. "What that means is only that he wasn't born in this state, not under that name, anyway."

MaryBeth gazed intently at Butz. "I thought the police were badly overworked?"

"We are that."

"You seem to be spending a lot of time and energy trying to find out about a man you concede hasn't even committed a chargeable crime."

Butz gave a choking little combination laugh and cough. "When you've been in this business as long as I have, you get hunches, instincts about people. Little hairs on the back of my neck stand straight up when something isn't kosher."

MaryBeth flashed Gray a curious warning look, but didn't interrupt.

"I've got one of my feelings about Mr. Sprat," he continued. "Hairs bristling from the first time I ever met the son-of-a… Well, you get the picture.

"I told Ms. Flowers there wasn't anything I could do, but I have kind of kept my eyes open, and I have done a little digging to see what I might be able to turn up. Plus, I ran across a couple of other little wrinkles before I took a look and noticed Mrs. Sprat putting on so much weight…"

"You met Mrs. Sprat?" MaryBeth interrupted.

Butz gestured with the cigar between the fingers of his left hand. "I made it a point to get a look at her right after I interviewed her sister, and every couple of weeks after that. When I saw she was putting on serious poundage, well, you know, the bristling hairs on my neck," he interrupted himself. "Let's just say I was pretty well convinced Sprat was up to something."

Wheeler cleared his throat. "Is Sprat a CPA? An accountant of any kind?"

"He has one of those certificates you get from a mail order outfit in West Virginia." Butz's grin came out more of a grimace. "It was good enough to get him into Younger and Zale during tax season a couple of years ago when they were pressed and needed an extra hand. I guess he worked out well enough for them. They think the world of him."

MaryBeth said, "You've talked to his boss?"

"Casually, at the golf course one morning. Before

he teed off. A secretary tipped me that he'd be there. I dressed the part, and we had what you might call a conversation in passing. I said I'd met an employee of his, Jack Sprat, and had been impressed with the fellow. Planned to see if he could help streamline the accounting for my business. The man said Sprat would be ideal for the job, but they'd fight to keep him."

Gray couldn't restrain himself any longer. "I'd say Sprat has certainly adept at juggling figures, if his wife is an example of his work." Gray laughed boisterously at first, noticing, then slowly acknowledging the somber disapproval on the faces of his two companions.

Butz put the cigar back in his mouth, then quickly pulled it out again.

In an effort to fill the awkward silence and perhaps redeem himself, Gray tried again. "I've heard of kiting checks but kiting wives is a brand new slant."

MaryBeth and Butz groaned in unison.

"If there is a crime in all this, it's going to be damn hard to prove," Butz said, frustration and disappointment deepening the lines in his face.

MaryBeth stepped in front of Butz and looked directly into his somber countenance. "What do you mean?"

He returned her gaze. "I'm saying that overdosing someone on kindness is not illegal. I'm saying that I can find absolutely nothing criminal in what Sprat is doing, or has done, with or to his wife. I'm hanging out here on my day off to witness what may be a homicide, and I'm not lifting a pinkie to stop it."

He jammed the cold cigar back in his mouth and dusted a couple of pieces of tobacco off his bottom lip.

"I had an independent auditor go over Sprat's bank

accounts and unauthorized copies of his last two tax returns, which I appropriated, illegally, by the way." He gave them an apologetic glance. "As far as my guy could tell, Sprat looks clean as a whistle. Some questions I asked him turned up what might possibly be another angle to this thing."

"Tax returns!" Gray fairly shouted, again taking the situation seriously. "We can track him through his tax returns."

Shaking his head, Butz set his jaw. "There are no records of his filing one before 2006. The IRS started compiling records on computer in the eighties. Their records are a little sketchy up to 2006, on Sprat or anyone else."

Silenced, Gray drew a deep breath. A pall hung over the trio as each examined his own thoughts, mentally groping for a key to Sprat's mysteriously locked past.

"How about his first wife?" Gray asked finally, breaking the quiet. "Maybe we can find out more about him from her family or their mutual friends."

Butz's scowl deepened. "By 'his first wife,' you mean Swenson?"

"Who else?"

"I don't know." Butz looked as if he were being cagey. "It occurred to me that she may not have been his first wife."

MaryBeth caught his meaning and exhaled through her mouth, before she said, in a hushed voice, "You're saying there may have been others before her."

Gray looked from MaryBeth to Butz. "You think he's had others?"

"Hell, I don't know what he's done." The

speculations obviously had carried them into the detective's frustration zone. "Jack Sprat is a name out of a nursery rhyme. This guy may have come along and made him real. If he's into imaginary characters, he could have made Bluebeard real too, for all I know.

"I can tell you from years of experience, most criminals who find a modus operandi that works for them, stick with it. Some of them stick with stuff that doesn't work, thinking they'll make it work.

"Look at what we know about Sprat up to now: He's had two rich, older wives, at least old for a guy his age. It looks like both of them may be dead within a year after marrying him. There could be a long trail of deceased elderly wives, all of whom appeared to have died of natural causes. Why not? You've got to admit, it's a slick game. I got tipped to the scheme in progress, and I haven't got enough evidence to give the guy a parking ticket. A new wife every few years makes for several dead ladies by the time a guy's thirty-six, if he's as energetic and efficient as our guy appears to be.

"I have always been a believer in that adage about there being nothing original under the sun, particularly in crime, but Sprat, here, may have come up with a new twist to an old game. If he has, then, so far, I don't have one damn idea about how to stop him."

Chapter Nine
Conundrum

The three companions were quiet for several moments before MaryBeth spoke, staring at Butz. "What other little angle are you looking at?"

"Huh?"

"You said asking him some questions turned up something you thought might be another angle to this case."

Butz allowed a grudging smile. "You caught that, did you?" He hesitated, as if rethinking something. "Your client and her sister, at one time, had a younger sibling. This little sister had a son, a ne'er-do-well, raised rich, spoiled to money as a kid. He's run through everything his parents left him and has been scanning about for a new source of income. Rich relatives like a couple of old aunties probably look like possibilities, at least one whose fortune is still intact, plus earnings."

"You mean Clover Sprat," MaryBeth said softly.

"She was the most obvious relative still sitting on a pile of family funds. You could see how he might think he deserved a share of hers, eventually. At age forty-one, he may be getting impatient, cooling his heels waiting to outlive the old girl."

MaryBeth's expression clouded. "Didn't Clover have relatives other than her sister Treena and some grasping nephew?"

"You mean relatives, not counting an ominous spouse, of course."

She winced. "Yes, naturally, Clover had Jack. Does this nephew live or work anywhere around here? Is he close enough to be aware of her current situation?"

Butz put the gnawed end of his cold cigar in his mouth and clamped his jaws, then talked around it. "He relocated about the time Clover married Jack. Didn't just come back to the state, but settled right here in town. Not in a classy apartment in midtown, of course, but a modest studio setup downtown."

"Oh." MaryBeth's shoulders slumped as she nodded. Her obvious distress prompted Butz to continue.

"Now see here, miss, I'm trying to look at this thing objectively, from different perspectives. For instance, what if Mrs. Sprat originally named this ne'er-do-well nephew—whose name, by the way, is Wayne Tessler—made him a primary heir in her will?"

"Named him her heir, not her sister?"

"It sounded to me as if Wayne Tessler and Treena Flowers might have come in for an equal amount of cash and property, in Mrs. Sprat's original will. At least that's what a woman at the law office hinted. I think the person I spoke with told me as much as she felt client privilege allowed. A younger sister to Treena and Clover was already deceased at the time their father died. In accordance with their father's will, their little sister's share was split between the old man's two surviving offspring, Treena and Clover. I imagine Nephew Tessler was pissed..." Butz gave MaryBeth a startled look and cleared his throat as if trying to erase his crude remark from the air.

She smiled and shook her head slightly, mutely denying that she was offended.

Butz looked relieved and continued speaking. "Tessler may have expected to inherit something from his aunts' wills. One or both may have told him so, at least have hinted that he was an heir. An effort to keep peace in the family. Clover's former accountant—before Sprat, that is—told me Clover paid for the nephew's college—six years of it. Maybe he has plans to inherit something from both his aunties. I don't know how he reacted when he found out about the Sprats' marriage. He could have gotten that information from the newspaper. If he expected to be an heir, Wayne might be savvy enough to realize Clover could change her beneficiaries, once she had a husband. He might be involved with a scheme to keep that from happening, might be following along with someone else's plan, or might have ideas of his own, especially after he observed Mrs. Sprat's physical condition."

"So, you think the nephew came back to spy on his aunts?"

"No idea, but the timing for his move back to town suggests something." Butz chewed the cigar as MaryBeth frowned down at the carpet and began to pace.

Gray continued to stand in one spot, his eyes darting from the lieutenant to MaryBeth and back again. Finally, he mused out loud. "I wonder if Sprat's other wife had a broken leg."

"If she did, nobody noticed it, or didn't think it significant enough to mention it on her death certificate," Butz said. "I asked about that specifically. No one at the hospital could remember details of her treatment, a natural death all those years ago, only what was written down. I tried everyone, from the doctor who signed her death certificate to her family physician, to relatives. Of course, the family may have been in shock or upset. I doubt the physicians looked for or noticed anything unusual in her physical condition. One nurse noted she was 'morbidly obese.'

"No one suspected anything sinister. Cremated her. She was a hefty, fifty-seven-year-old woman, and she died suddenly. Embolism or aneurysm, stroke or heart. Lot of women—men, too—in that age group died that year. Lot of them are doing the same thing now, most of them passing without causing a stir beyond their own immediate circle."

MaryBeth and Gray both nodded before she fairly exploded with a new thought. "If you don't have evidence of any criminal activity, what are you doing here?"

"Like I told you, those little hairs on the back of my neck just won't lie down. I'm here for them, trying to make myself believe that no one's perpetrating a crime right in front of my nose."

Gray looked sympathetic. "That self-convincing thing: are you doing any good with it?"

Butz focused grudging attention on the other man and said, "I'm doing. I don't know if it's any good or not. If I keep at it, though, something will turn up before I quit it. Usually does."

Gray directed the detective's attention to MaryBeth. "She may be able to turn up something tomorrow." He wanted to inject some encouragement into their little group. "She's having lunch with Larry Simonovsky down at the *Times*. He's digging up some info for her on Leland Jack Sprat."

"Lunch? At noon?"

Gray nodded.

"Where are you going to be about that time of day, Wheeler?" Butz flicked the end of the cold cigar with his thumb, sending a shower of cold ashes to the carpeted floor. He scuffed them to invisibility with the heel of his shoe.

"I'll probably hang around the lobby at the *Times*, just in case Larry comes up with something she's not prepared to handle." Gray said the words suggestively, arching his eyebrows to indicate they had special meaning.

MaryBeth frowned at him. "I'm a big girl, Wheeler. Like most females, I've had some training and experience at hand-to-hand."

Gray stared at her and his voice dropped to a dare. "Yeah? Well, this tingling business—ants in the pants and prickling hairs on the back of a person's neck—is new to you. If Larry turns up some big news about Sprat, it might make you start tingling and chilling and you'd mistake it for love. I want to be around to help you avoid any misinterpretations."

Butz gave the pair a quick grin but sobered again just as quickly. "I want to know what you find out." He spoke directly to MaryBeth, who nodded, indicating she would relay whatever information she got. "By the way, how did you happen to ask me if Sprat's earlier wife had a broken leg?"

Gray picked up the verbal gauntlet, drawing Butz' attention. "Ah, yes. Well, the good doctor mentioned that Clover Sprat has a broken right tibia. You may have noticed that Clover baby was not into soccer or horseshoes, or any recreational effort that might have gotten her a broken leg. A nurse noticed the break by chance, the doc said."

Butz scowled as if he didn't catch Gray's meaning. "What does a broken tibia have to do with anything?"

"Nothing much," Gray said, pretending to be only slightly interested in his own response, "except the doc said that is what's going to kill her."

Butz put the cigar back in his mouth, as if preventing his own questions, encouraging Gray to continue.

"He said she might have had a chance if she'd just had the stroke or whatever, but emboli hiding in the bones escape when a bone is broken. In this case, it's the emboli cluttering up her already-overcrowded circulation system that is going to make her croak. He said that broken leg is the final nail in her coffin."

Butz studied him quietly, then removed the cigar from his mouth. "How did she break the leg?"

MaryBeth eased onto one of the chapel pews but sat erectly. "The doctor doesn't know. As far as we know, no one's mentioned it to Sprat yet, either."

Wheeler cut a questioning look at Butz. "You didn't happen to find any old baseball bats lying around when you searched their apartment, did you, Butz?"

The lieutenant cast him a dark look. "What makes you think we searched their apartment?"

For the first time, Wheeler was at a loss for words.

"You're right," Butz continued, frowning into Wheeler's face. "Not only that we searched, but that there was a baseball bat. Two rookie patrolmen with me probably got their prints all over it."

Butz sat down in the pew beside MaryBeth and

continued. "What's the difference? You'd expect a man's fingerprints to be on his own baseball bat, wouldn't you?"

"Wouldn't be anything incriminating about that," Gray agreed, sliding into the pew on the other side of MaryBeth.

Butz drew a deep breath and leaned back as if he were tired. "This guy is good. We'll check the bat. Might be lint from her gown, which could be circumstantial evidence that he slugged his wife right outta this park. We'll follow every hint of a lead. All these guys slip up sooner or later. We have just got to stay on 'em."

Gray, too, slouched against the back of the pew. "I think so far his only mistake has been marrying Treena Flowers' sister. Treena's the one who sicced all three of us on him."

Butz nodded. "I wonder if she's here now. I might go have a look around, maybe get a word with her; express my sympathy and ask for details. Wouldn't have to let on I'm investigating or anything. I might tell her I'm up here with family and just passing the time." Butz stood, without enthusiasm.

"She's pretty sharp, Lieutenant," Gray said. "Watch yourself. Be subtle. If she thinks you have an official interest, she may unload on you. and you could be here all day."

"Right." Butz strolled to the door. He looked back as he opened it. "Thanks." He pushed through and was gone.

MaryBeth and Gray, side-by-side on the chapel pew, smiled mutely, first at the doors through which Butz had disappeared, then at each other.

Chapter Ten
Reconnoitering

MaryBeth Gilland and Gray Wheeler stepped from the elevator into the hallway leading to Your Eyes Only Detective Agency. Neither spoke. They looked straight ahead as they walked, each immersed in his own thoughts. Lights were on in the office, despite the fact it was well after five.

"A penny for your thoughts," Gray said, breaking the silence as he pushed open the office door, then stepped aside to let her pass.

"Hot bath."

"What?"

"I'm thinking of a hot bath."

Gray inhaled as she squeezed by him and glided into the office leaving him to occupy the doorway alone.

"It was good for me," he said. "Was it good for you?" He didn't wait for her answer. "A hot bath, huh? Yeah, that sounds good to me, too."

She grimaced. "Alone, Wheeler. I bathe strictly alone." She smiled at Ms. Yehle as the older woman, reading glasses clinging to the slightly bulbed end of her nose, returned to the reception room from Wheeler's office.

He motioned MaryBeth toward the open door to his office and followed.

"Do you really think you should?" he asked, closing the door and picking up the conversation. "Right in the middle of a possible murder case with your nerves tingling…"

"They're raw." She sank into the chair Treena Flowers had filled so abundantly that morning.

He sat on the corner of his desk, studying her with a taunting smile. "The ants are marching. Your muscles are flexed to the ready. A hot bath might dull that professional edge."

She slipped her feet out of her heels and buried her toes in the carpet, wincing and groaning with what Gray could not decide was pain or pleasure. He allowed her an opportunity to tell him which.

"If I get a hot bath and sleep, I'll hit the floor tomorrow morning alert, ready for anything," she said. "Without the bath, the sleep, a change of clothing—especially these shoes—I'll be sluggish and bleary. My judgment will be muddled."

"Muddled?" Gray mouthed the word, musing. "That has a nice sound to it. I think I'd like you muddled. Maybe even knee-walking muddled."

"Not likely that will happen." She smiled into his eyes. "There are some people around whom a woman cannot afford to get that kind of muddled."

A quick rap at the door announced Ms. Yehle, who arrived notebook in hand and eyeglasses secured nearer the bridge of her nose.

"Ah, Ms. Yehle." Gray stood and waved her into a chair.

The secretary ignored his gesture and remained standing.

"What life-threatening emergency has reared its

ugly head in our absence?"

"There have been several." The furrows between her eyes deepened as she peered into the notebook and her eyeglasses crept down her nose.

Gray looked surprised. "Really?" He walked to her side and tried to decipher the notebook, glanced toward MaryBeth and shrugged, then returned to his perch on the corner of his desk to await the translation.

"The copying machine quit," Mrs. Yehle intoned with what sounded like reverence.

Gray arched a brow, pretending concern. "Without giving two weeks notice?"

She ignored him. "It has been behaving a little erratically lately. That should have tipped me. I should have looked into the matter. I guess the pressure of our workload was just too much for it."

He gave her a slight smile. "That's the life-threatening emergency we're talking about?"

"Well, that's certainly one of them." She appeared undeterred. "Then a salesman called to say we are paying too much to rent the other telephone company's equipment when we could purchase theirs cheaper, but we would have to act before six p.m. tonight or miss their special sale deadline." Suddenly her eyes rounded and engaged his. "Wheeler, deadlines rattle me."

She removed the glasses and stared into Gray's face. "It's a quarter after five now. All afternoon the hands on the clock have ticked off the minutes, relentlessly. I didn't know if you'd be back in time as the deadline loomed ever closer. Do you have any idea what kind of pressure that puts on someone in my position?"

The formerly unflappable Ms. Yehle began fanning

herself with the notebook.

"Then the tax man called." She drew several quick, nervous breaths. "He said it's time for cost-of-living raises, and he wanted to know if you wanted retirement programs or lower-deductible health insurance or raises or what?"

Suddenly she moved several steps and sank into the chair he had offered originally. Dropping her notebook in her lap, she curled her shoulders and stretched her legs straight out in front of her.

Gray looked at MaryBeth, the corners of his mouth twitching. "MaryBeth, I ask you, are these matters worthy of the attention of a company's top executive? I am trained to handle life-and-death situations, but copying machines and telephones and cost-of-living increases take all the fun out of being C.E.O."

MaryBeth leaned forward. "Ms. Yehle, what is that Dorothy Lyng working on right now?"

Both Gray and Ms. Yehle regarded her curiously.

Yehle looked at Gray, then back at MaryBeth and sat straighter. "She just finished with the Wellington divorce matter and is scheduled to begin McDaniel in the morning."

MaryBeth looked at Gray. "Could we ask Ms. Lyng to follow Leland Sprat tonight?"

He shrugged and looked to Ms. Yehle.

"She's been out every night club hopping behind that Wellington character," Ms. Yehle said.

MaryBeth stood, without putting on her shoes. "She can doze in the hospital lobby, and we'll be sure to know if Sprat goes anywhere."

Gray smiled and nodded. "Good idea. You're getting into this, and Lyng is perfect. Sprat will never spot her."

MaryBeth looked satisfied. "Also, do we pay for a service contract on the copier?"

Ms. Yehle nodded and almost smiled at the words. "Of course. Yes, we do." Yehle sighed and her face brightened with an adoring look at MaryBeth. "Of course. We might as well get some good out of it."

Encouraged by their responses, MaryBeth folded her arms and began to stride, pacing the office as if entertaining great thoughts. "About the phones: let's keep what we've got another couple of weeks." She gave Yehle a direct look. "Put the brochures on my desk. I'll go over them and then make an informed decision."

Ms. Yehle turned all the way around looking for MaryBeth's imagined desk. When her spin brought her face-to-face with Gray, he winked, grinned, and nodded. Ms. Yehle gave him an answering nod of understanding and jotted a note. MaryBeth did not seem to notice the exchange.

"Finally," MaryBeth said, still pacing, "canvass the employees. Find out if our people want a retirement program or better health insurance or raises or what would best serve them."

"Of course," Ms. Yehle said again, gazing at MaryBeth with what appeared to be adoration before speaking quietly to herself. "We'll let them decide."

Gray stirred. "Sounds fair."

Ms. Yehle turned to Gray. "Oh, yes, sir, totally, completely and brilliantly fair." She drew a deep, cleansing breath before she spoke again. "Oh, Mr. Wheeler, it's such a relief to have such a strong hand at the helm, making decisions and steering us out of the sea of confusion."

She repositioned her glasses, pushing them from the end of her nose back to the bridge of that feature before both she and Gray turned admiring looks toward MaryBeth, the person mutually regarded as the "strong hand at the helm."

Grinning toward his new protégée, Gray said, "Yes, Ms. Yehle, it certainly is. She's definitely impressive."

When Ms. Yehle stood, smoothed her skirt and left Gray and MaryBeth alone in the office, neither of them spoke. MaryBeth refused to meet Gray's gaze. Still shoeless, she paced to the window, did a double-take at the non view, and strode back to the center of the office, tapping her fingernails on her teeth and studiously avoiding his eyes. Circling the room a couple of rounds, eventually she eased into her chair to retrieve her shoes. "I have a strong incentive tonight."

"Big bucks?" Gray asked, still propped at the corner of the desk, pivoting to follow her pacing.

"Hot bath. Good night, Mr. Wheeler." She gathered her purse and stood, brushing the front of her skirt, mimicking Ms. Yehle.

He, too, stood, never taking his eyes off her. "How about dinner?"

She walked toward the door without acknowledging the invitation but he wasn't willing to let it go. "Your place? My place? Some place? The bath you mentioned: a nice Jacuzzi somewhere?"

Without looking back, she enunciated clearly. "No thank you. I will be back here at the crack of dawn tomorrow morning, spanking clean, alert, and ready for action. Can you beat a deal like that?"

"Yeah." He intended his whispery tone to leave no doubt as to his meaning. "All night long."

"Not with me, you can't." Still without turning around, she held up one hand silencing him and signaling good-bye, leaving the door ajar as she made her exit.

Watching from behind her receptionist's station as MaryBeth left, Ms. Yehle did not take her eyes off of her as the newest employee floated through the reception room door and out into the corridor. Yehle drew and released a deep breath and spoke audibly enough for Gray to hear her say, "MaryBeth Gilland, you are something else."

When MaryBeth had been gone two or three minutes, Ms. Yehle folded her notebook. "Good night, Mr. Wheeler," she called. "It's been an amazing day." She peeped in at him as the telephone began ringing. He didn't want to hear either the phone or Yehle's voice. He wanted to bask in the fragrance wafting about his office. A new, exotic scent that aroused…instincts.

Gray walked around his desk, fingering a paperweight shaped like a whale, trying to recall if he had ever seen it before.

He picked up a pencil, peering hard at the sharpened lead, then gently laid it down and ignored the telephone, which stopped on the fourth ring.

He began humming and sat down in his chair, put his fingertips together, and clicked the nails of his index fingers against his front teeth. When he realized what he was humming, he chuckled to himself and began mouthing the words to the song. "What a difference a day makes…" Smiling, he rocked back in his chair.

"Mr. Wheeler, I've got Ms. Lyng on the phone,"

Yehle said over the intercom. "She wants you to describe Mr. Sprat so she can locate him."

Grinning, Gray said, "Tell her to take the night off. I probably wouldn't get much sleep anyway. I'll keep an eye on our Mr. Sprat myself."

He thought he detected a slight giggle in Yehle's voice as she said, "I'll tell her."

Chapter Eleven
Tail

In his shirtsleeves, Wheeler squirmed in the molded plastic chair and stretched. Reaching both arms, fists clenched, high over his head, he yawned. Positioned in the waiting area near the elevators on the eighth floor, he had an unobstructed view of Room 817.

The lobby clock above the chairs directly across from him read 11:03 when a muscular man slipped out of the room and eased the door closed behind him. Gray squinted. He arched his eyebrows, an effort to force his eyes to open wider. He wanted to look like he was struggling to stay awake. The glimpse of Sprat on the move made his stomach churn with anticipation. Taking special notice of the size of Sprat's hands—noticeably small—and his arms, short in relation to the man's body, Wheeler bit back a smile.

Sprat wore an expensive dark suit which bound a little through the shoulders. Some guys had them tailored like that for effect, Wheeler mused. Through narrowed eyes, Gray studied his subject up and down from his perfectly coifed hair to the high sheen of patent leather shoes.

Sprat didn't look around, didn't appear to notice Wheeler or either of the other two people in the waiting area. Instead, the grieving husband walked briskly to the elevator. When the elevator doors closed and Sprat was gone, Wheeler jumped up, grabbed his jacket off the coat tree and slipped it on as he ran through the door marked "Stairs."

Leaping two and three stairs at a time, stumbling, righting himself, then galloping again, Wheeler reached the main floor, slammed through the doors, and bolted for his car. He was snapping the seat belt before Sprat stepped off the elevator with three other people, clearly visible through the glassed front of the hospital.

Wheeler had located Sprat's car earlier. In spite of the fact his sports car was parked in the hospital lot, the man hailed a cab.

Allowing plenty of traffic between his car and the cab, Wheeler tailed it to Bonicellis Theater and Supper Club. He pulled into parking on the street as Sprat paid the cabby and went inside.

Ducking into the vestibule of the posh dinner club, Wheeler grabbed up a house phone, got a dial tone, and punched in her number, which he had memorized only that morning.

"MaryBeth?" he said softly into the receiver. "Gray Wheeler here. Sprat's moving. I'm on him but this isn't the kind of place a guy goes by himself without drawing attention. Would you consider...?" He jerked the phone away from his ear.

"You've been a model," he argued after her initial objections became quiet grumbling. "Dab on some make-up. Get a different look. He probably won't recognize you anyway. Okay, use whatever camouflage you want. We are at Bonicellis on Armbruster. I'll get us a table." He paused to listen. "Yes, a table in the back. Nobody will even know we're here. Hurry."

Feeling a little smug to get such a hot date on short

notice, he went inside. Oh, yeah, he liked this. Waiting around for MaryBeth Gilland was the way he would enjoy spending a lot of his time. He asked the hostess for a table for two in a dark corner. She led him to a booth near the kitchen doors. When his eyes adjusted, he scanned the room and spotted Sprat sitting with an attractive blonde who looked remarkably like MaryBeth Gilland. Wheeler studied the pair a long moment reassuring himself the woman was not MaryBeth. He might not have been convinced if he hadn't just called his new associate on the telephone at her place.

Two empty drink glasses on the table in front of him gave mute testimony to the full hour Wheeler had been waiting, when a tall, bespectacled woman with short, dark hair approached his table. She wore flats, a high-collar blouse and a drab A-line skirt.

"I'm not ready for another one yet," Gray said, without looking at the woman.

"Move over," she whispered. "It's me."

Looking up, Gray gasped. "I said disguise yourself, not desecrate yourself." He scrutinized her, dumbfounded.

Sliding into the booth beside him, her eyes darted about the room. "I didn't want him to recognize me."

"I didn't recognize you." He felt more than disappointed. More like devastated.

She frowned as she spotted Sprat. "Good."

"Surely it didn't take you all this time to come out looking this bad."

When she suddenly made eye contact, her manner more than her expression altered his attitude. He squared his shoulders and tried a reassuring, though faltering, smile. "But then I guess it probably takes a lot more time and effort to camouflage natural good looks like yours."

She huffed. "I called Mrs. Flowers to bring her up to speed." She focused her attention for a moment on Sprat and his lady friend. "And don't call me 'Shirley.'"

He scrambled mentally for a meaning to that comment before he caught it. He brightened and snorted a quick laugh at her little joke. She was referring, of course, to his saying, "Surely it didn't take you all that time…"

Disguised though she was, he recognized a smile as her full lips, which currently appeared amazingly thin, tilted upward at each end. She liked that he caught her little joke. Obviously she was more than just a pretty face…an angelic face…and an astonishing figure…and… It was a bonus, her being mentally quick, as well.

While he entertained wistful thoughts, she said, "I thought you assigned Ms. Lyng to watch him tonight." Before he could explain, she plunged ahead. "What're you doing here? What's he doing here?" She took another quick glance at their prey. "That woman he's with…she looks something like me, don't you think? Who is she? Do you know who she is?"

"She doesn't look anything like you look now." He frowned into her face. "She does look like you look when you look like you." He couldn't take his eyes off of her, studying her up and down again. "No, I don't know the woman he's with. But then that's not so surprising. I don't even know the woman I'm with." Gray signaled the waitress. "Dorothy Lyng was tired. I felt stimulated, so I took the duty. As to what he's doing here, it looks to me like he's come for a little R and R after hardship duty."

MaryBeth suddenly bent her head, turning her face to the wall on her left. She put her elbows on the table and propped her head with both hands.

Sprat was looking their direction, trying to summon the waitress.

"I think he just asked his lady to dance." MaryBeth immediately slid out of the booth. "Come on."

Gray stood and caught her hand. Glancing casually around the room, she clutched Gray's hand and trailed him to the small dance floor.

He eased her into his arms. "You're shorter." He turned them so her back was to Sprat which seemed to encourage her to look at him. "It's the shoes."

"Yeah." He breathed in the now familiar fragrance of her. "Hmmm." He closed his eyes.

"Are you watching him?" she asked, retreating a step to glower at Gray. "Are you paying attention?"

"Absolutely." He swept a token glance toward the pair across the floor.

"They sure dance close if they are supposed to have just met." MaryBeth craned her neck trying to see the couple behind her.

Closing his eyes, Gray hummed his agreement. She jostled him. When he looked at her, his eyes rounded and he grimaced. The music hadn't stopped, but Gray turned her toward their table wordlessly.

"What's the matter with you?" MaryBeth whispered as he led her to the booth.

He couldn't bring himself to look at her. "Why?"

"You leered at me all day. I know that hungry look. I figured I would have to fight you off if we were ever together after dark. So, here we are alone on the dance floor, slow music, you've had a long, hard day and a couple of drinks. I just expected to have to…well, you know…arm wrestle."

He put her in the booth first and stood looking down at her a long moment before he slid in beside her.

"The leering was admiration, when you were you. Now, you're somebody else. You were a princess in the daylight and a haggard stepsister after dark. That's not the way the fairy tale goes."

MaryBeth's jaw muscles tightened. "You mean the only part of me you can admire is the physical part?" Her voice sounded cold, brittle.

He sat straighter, alert to her annoyed expression and inflection. "That is so not fair and you know it."

"Let me tell you something, Mr. Gray Wheeler, there's a lot more to me than my outside physical appearance."

"I know that."

"What if I were mutilated in a car accident?"

"I'd send flowers."

"But you wouldn't breathe through your mouth and stare slack-jawed and welcome me into your office and into your life, isn't that right? What if I had looked like this when I walked into the agency today?"

Gray cleared his throat and took a sip of his drink. It was watery. He needed a fresh one, especially if he was going to be doing verbal combat with this…woman. "Would you like something to drink?" he asked, looking around for the waitress.

MaryBeth was not to be deterred. "What if I looked like this all the time? Would you have called, invited me to meet you here?"

He shrugged. "I don't know."

"Would you have asked Dorothy Lyng to join you?"

"No."

"What you are saying is that our new association is based entirely on my looks?"

"I wouldn't say entirely. No."

Her jaw muscles flexed. "But it is a major consideration, isn't it?" Her words seethed from between pinched, camouflaged lips.

Staring at those lips, he stiffened. "Let's put this shoe on another foot. How about you?"

She started to retort, then hesitated. "How about me, what?"

"Doesn't how I look influence how you feel about me?"

Her eyes got rounder and seemed to shoot sparks as she bumped him, indicating she wanted him to move and let her out. "No, I'd dislike you the same, tall or short, fat or thin, in color, black-and-white, cinemascope or with full stereophonic accompaniment."

He slid out of her way and she exploded out of the booth, turned on her heel and strode quickly toward the exit.

Gray put money on the table and followed.

She was gone when he reached the door at precisely the same time Jack Sprat and Sprat's companion got there. Gray stepped back and held the door for the couple, then followed them out.

MaryBeth backed out of her parking space, wheels squealing. Adjusting her mirror, she saw Sprat and his lady friend. She spun forward, then jammed on her brakes. Her car lurched to a stop in the middle of the circle drive, blocking the cab Sprat hailed.

His fares secure, the cabby honked for MaryBeth to move her car, then honked again when she didn't respond. Then he leaned on his horn. MaryBeth sat as if she hadn't a care in the world watching in her rearview as Wheeler jogged to his car.

Engine started, Wheeler careened from his parking place, made a U-turn and glided into the circle drive, joining the line of traffic stalled behind the cab and MaryBeth.

When Wheeler was in position, MaryBeth pulled aside, allowing the cab and the cars behind to pass, then she followed.

The three vehicles, the cab, followed by Wheeler, with MaryBeth's vehicle bringing up the rear, formed a conga line as they paraded to a high-rise apartment building near the hospital. The cab dropped Sprat and his friend. MaryBeth continued following as Gray parked at the curb half a block beyond.

Wheeler walked back to MaryBeth's car. As he approached, she locked the doors. He circled to the driver's side. Without looking at him, she cracked the window so she could hear.

"Unlock the doors," he said quietly. "You're being very immature."

"Immature? That's comical, coming from you."

"If you don't open this door, I'll just get the spare key and open it myself."

She looked startled. "What spare key?"

"The one in the little magnetic box in the wheel well." She tapped the unlock, and he strode quickly around to the passenger side and got in.

She frowned at him. "How did you know about the spare key in the box in the wheel well?"

He shrugged. "I didn't know about it, but efficient people sometimes hide one there and I figured you for one of those excessively cautious ladies who might have. It was a lucky guess." He gave her what he hoped was a disarmingly boyish grin.

MaryBeth sighed. "Sometimes you make me absolutely furious. You've done it several times today and I don't even know you that well."

His boyish smile broadened. "Oh, yeah? Why, do you suppose I push your buttons?"

Her eyes narrowed as she caught the note of merriment in his voice. "I suppose it's because you're so superficial."

"This, coming from a woman who's made her living in the false image business for years?"

"What are you trying to say?"

"You women have bathed and oiled yourselves for hundreds—even thousands—of years, to entice men," Gray said matter-of-factly. "Then, having spent all that time and money and energy, you act surprised when males are attracted to your soft, sweet-smelling bodies, and you hit us with a load of rhetorical crap about wanting us to love you for your real selves—the woman within. Ha!"

When he looked at her, he couldn't help smiling. Slowly, trying to appear as non threatening as possible, he used both hands to remove her phony eyeglasses.

"You really are beautiful." He crooned the words as he carefully tugged the dark wig, releasing her blonde curls. She shook her head and riffled her fingers through those golden tresses. He continued in a low croon.

"Today you caught me standing deaf and blind when you walked into my office. Could I help it that I was dazzled, so swept off my feet that I forgot to inquire about your I.Q.? I didn't care if you had an I.Q. when you so obviously have everything else.

"When you asked for a job, I levitated. The rest of the day I anticipated getting up in the mornings from now on excited about going to the office, about seeing you, breathing you, talking to you, being with you."

He caught the end of the tie securing her blouse collar and tugged. The bow slid undone. When she didn't move or object, he unbuttoned the first three buttons and laid her shirt collar back.

"All day long, my heart's beat this jungle rhythm. Then you show up here tonight, like this. Didn't you think I'd notice? Didn't you think I would be disappointed? Crushed. Maybe even object?"

She flinched a little as he smoothed her hair. "I appreciate your dedication, your sense of humor, your intellect. But mostly, I appreciate your gorgeous, sweet-smelling, sexy body. Surely, you can't be mad at me for that."

She smiled but before she could speak, he added. "Sorry, I know you don't like for me to call you 'Shirley.'"

"No, I really don't mind." Her voice sounded huskier than it had. "I do understand. I guess it was Mrs. Neanderthal's body that kept Mr. Neanderthal under control. But, there have been times today, Mr. Wheeler, when you have behaved astonishingly like Mr. Neanderthal."

Gazing into her face, Gray leaned toward her.

Suddenly her head jerked back and she looked frightened. "Here he comes."

"Mr. Neanderthal?"

"Sprat."

Gray slid his left arm along the back of the seat behind MaryBeth and leaned close so that his lips were near her ear. "If we hold our positions, he'll never notice us. What's he doing?"

Gray pressed his lips to her throat, allowing her an unobstructed view of Sprat.

She leaned forward a little to see around Gray. "He's hailing a cab."

Gray nibbled kisses along her collarbone. "Now, what's he doing?"

"He's leaving. Gray, he's getting away."

"That's okay. Now what?"

"Wheeler," she said shoving his shoulders, "he's gone."

"Well, don't just sit there. Drive, woman. Follow him."

She started the engine and snapped it into gear. "What about your car?"

"I'll pick it up later. Go."

MaryBeth kept the cab in sight as they followed Sprat to the hospital. They parked and watched him walk to his Mercedes, get in, and drive it from the parking lot.

"Do you think he's going home?" MaryBeth asked.

Admiring her profile, Gray nodded. "Hmmm."

"Do we know who the girl is?"

He shrugged and arched his eyebrows. "We know where she lives and what she looks like. We can find out who she is. Right now we need to get you home. I'll get out here and take a cab back to my car."

"Are you sure?"

"Yes." He walked to the driver's side and she lowered her window.

"Do you want to kiss me good night?" she asked, a note of skepticism in her voice.

He flashed the boyish grin. "Thanks all the same, I think I'll pass."

Looking a little puzzled, she returned the smile. "Shall we shake hands then?"

"Next time."

"Then good night, Mr. Wheeler." She started the engine.

He watched the tail lights of her car until they were out of sight. Humming, he hailed a cab.

Chapter Twelve
Near Miss

MaryBeth stepped off the elevator and looked both ways before she walked to the door marked "Library."

Her casual clothing and the picnic hamper she carried looked out of place in the stuffy solemnity of the corridor. The neck of a wine bottle protruded from the top of the basket, propping the lid open.

Just as she reached the opaque glass door, Larry Simonovsky threw it open. He wore neatly pressed slacks and a stiffly new shirt, fold marks still visible. His hair was combed and he stood erect, to his full height, as he smiled down at her appreciatively and reached for the picnic basket.

"Hello," MaryBeth said, returning the smile and relinquishing the basket.

"Welcome to my parlor, my lovely."

"Thank you, but that sounds a little ominous. Isn't that what the spider said to the fly?"

"Hmmm," he sighed. "I believe it is."

She followed him into the musty chamber. "Have you come up with any new information on our subject?"

"Yes, I have, but you'll have to coax it out of me." He eyed her suggestively as he closed the door and flipped the deadbolt.

She tried to ignore the implied threat. "I brought

along a little encouragement." She tapped the bottle with her fingernail. "Give me a hint about what you found."

He motioned her to take a chair at the table and she complied. He set the basket on the table, which obviously had been recently cleared and scrubbed. "In 2005, Jack Sprat was not."

"Was not what?" She twisted to keep her eyes on his face as he lifted the gingham napkin beneath the lid and began to examine the contents of the picnic hamper.

"Not. As in, was not in existence. That's the year he appeared. Until then he was not."

"How can that be?" She assumed the man was being cryptic on purpose. Teasing her to hold her attention. He certainly had that. She stood up again.

"Probably because until then, he was somebody else." Larry glanced up to smile at her. She stiffened, her eyes locked on Larry's face.

"In 2006," he continued, "just after he came into being, Sprat drove an Am-Care ambulance, lived in a boarding house at 11494 Constitution and was heavily into competitive body building."

"Had he changed his name or just moved here from out-of-state or what?" She sounded as confused as she felt.

Larry arched his eyebrows and began nodding. "At that time, Leland Jack Sprat was a brand spanking new person."

"No wonder we couldn't find background on him," she muttered, speaking mostly to herself. "Do you know more? Did you find out what his name was before?" Without allowing him time to answer, she rushed on. "Were you able to find background information about him under his original name?"

Larry laughed. "Yes, yes, and yes."

"Well? Let's have it."

"My plan for this meeting does not include your asking and my providing easy answers without some wheedling on your part. Now let's see what inducements we might have here in our charming little basket."

MaryBeth drew a deep breath, pursed her lips and frowned, then reached into the basket and produced two plastic, stemmed wine glasses.

Watching her results, Larry's smile returned. He picked up a foil-wrapped package, opened it, and inhaled. "Ah, the fragrance is enticing. Tiny little triangular cucumber sandwiches, without crusts." He arched his brows in an evil way and cut his eyes at her. "Decadent."

He opened a second package. "Rectangular little pimento cheese sandwiches without crusts." He investigated further. "Sensual. And an apple. Biblical. Appropriate. Complete with an actual paring knife." He shot a look at her from the corners of his eyes. "Two individual little bags of chips. Very tidy. How about napkins? Did you think to bring us anything to blot our...lips?"

MaryBeth scowled at his suggestive choice of words. "I thought it was accommodating of me to remember salt and pepper."

Larry stepped close and put his arm around her shoulders. "We've got paper towels right there in the bathroom to serve as napkins. No problem. Hold a moment." He retreated through an unmarked door on the east wall of the office.

"Larry, please. I need a lot more than what you've given me so far."

Propping the bathroom door open with his foot as he retrieved paper towels, he said, "Well put, beautiful child. Right back at you. I've shared a tantalizing morsel with you. Now it's your turn…to share."

She walked to the open doorway. "I brought lunch."

"Thanks." As he came out of the bathroom, he stopped dead center in the doorway, forcing her to turn sideways, putting them face-to-face in the narrow portal.

"Go ahead," he said, indicating she should slide past as he remained unmoving in the doorway.

She couldn't move without scrubbing her body against his. "Larry, excuse me. I can't get by you."

He smirked, but didn't budge, studying her with a Cheshire Cat grin. Clamping her jaws, she slid by, forced to press her body firmly to his as he remained unmoving, except that he closed his eyes.

"Ahhh, the ambrosia of touch added to the already captivating aura of your fragrance, not to mention the enchanting menu." He inhaled deeply, then chuckled and followed her back to the table.

Larry folded the paper towels and placed them, overlapping the sheets to provide place mats as a table covering. MaryBeth laid the packages of sandwiches on the improvised linens, then picked up the champagne, which Larry immediately took from her hand.

"What was Sprat's name before it became Sprat, Larry?" she asked quietly.

"Do you have any idea of how marvelous you

smell? I love your essence and, of course, the way you move. You fairly float through this grubby old room. It's never looked or smelled this good—ever. Even the dust kitties levitate with enthusiasm in your presence." He snorted, a half laugh, half cough, and opened the bottle, then poured white wine into the two plastic goblets and handed one to her. He lifted his glass indicating a toast. She hesitated.

"To you and me and the kitties." Hovering above her, he looked deep into her eyes. "And our eventual levitation."

Sipping, gazing at her over the rim of the glass, he reached for her. He had long, narrow, artistic fingers and huge, trustworthy hands, therefore, MaryBeth stood unmoving as he stroked her hair. When she didn't object, he set his glass on the table and positioned himself squarely in front of her.

Placing one hand on each side of her face, he leaned so close that his breath tickled her ear as he whispered, "Kluz. K-L-U-Z. His name was Howard Kluz."

MaryBeth retreated a step. Larry continued holding her face firmly and gazing into her eyes.

"Would you care to sit down?" she asked.

"We can make ourselves more comfortable than that." He continued surveying her face. "There's a hide-a-bed in the back for just such occasions."

"So, you entertain here often?"

He barked a quick laugh at the ceiling. "Every chance I get. Want to see? Wait right here while I go get things ready in the back room...the lounge, we call it."

MaryBeth gave him her best dimpled smile and

nodded permission.

As he hurried off, disappearing behind the ranks of cabinets, she frowned and whispered, "I'm afraid I really can't wait."

She walked quickly to the bathroom, making all the noise she could as she crossed the hardwood floor, and slammed the door shut, though she remained outside the privy. Stealthily, she retraced her steps, running on tiptoe, soundlessly slipped through the outside door into the corridor.

The elevator doors stood open. She scurried down the hall, frowning her puzzlement at the open doors. She thought she heard a noise and glanced behind her. Nothing. Still she had an eerie feeling and broke into a trot.

As she reached the elevator's yawning doorway, she pulled up short and let out an astonished, "What in the world…"

The elevator car was not there. The doors stood open over an empty shaft.

MaryBeth caught either side of the doorway and looked down, horrified that she had almost flung herself into that cavernous opening.

Suddenly two hands clamped her shoulders from behind. At first she thought they belonged to someone attempting to prevent her fall, but as small fingers bit into her upper arms, a substantial body bumped her forward.

Ripping her fingernails, she scrabbled for a better hold on the doorway, before a second bump sent her hurtling into the empty elevator shaft.

MaryBeth shrieked as she dropped, but the momentum of the thrust propelled her directly into a plastic-encased collection of cables vertically traversing the emptiness.

Clawing, she snatched at the plastic tubing and her scream stopped, although it echoed up and down the shaft. She didn't have the strength to scream and hold onto the slick lifeline. She continued clawing at the bundled cables that felt as if they were wrapped in a rain slicker. Finally, she clamped her arms and legs around the packaged cables that connected the car below to the lift apparatus in the ceiling above.

The cable covering was thick but wet. And cold. And slippery. Scrambling to hold herself against the lifeline, she pressed her face to it and concentrated on trying to breathe. Inhale. Exhale. Think. Trying to focus, she risked a look down.

Big mistake.

The elevator car appeared to be at least two floors below. Even hanging on with arms and legs in death grips, every few seconds, she slipped. Inches. She squeezed tighter before she slid again. Trying to recover the loss, she shinnied up. Instead of gaining altitude, she oozed down another foot.

"Help!" she screamed. Her voice echoed hollowly in the shaft. "Someone, help! I'm here! In the elevator shaft."

She slipped again. Pressing her forehead to the cable for leverage, she squeezed harder with both feet and struggled to tighten her handhold, but even that little movement caused her to descend another dozen inches.

What would happen if she let herself slide? She urged her brain to step up. Most likely, if she allowed herself to descend, she would stop on the roof of the elevator car. Then she could possibly locate an opening and lower herself into the car. Once inside, she could safely ride the rest of the way to the lobby. She congratulated herself on her logical thinking, especially in these circumstances.

She relaxed her arms and eased her handhold on the cable, only slightly. She slid another couple of feet. Amazing. Her plan might be working. She relaxed her feet and legs only a little and slithered down, not smoothly, but slowly, at first. All of her strength and her mental concentration centered on clinging to the cable. Her slide gained momentum. She tightened her grasp in an attempt to slow herself but, as before, tightening her grip seemed to make her drop faster. The dark, musty shaft became more frightening as she sank, further from the light from the door at the opening now high overhead.

She didn't dare look up, yet she had an eerie feeling—a premonition almost—that murderous eyes were watching from above. She dug her fingernails into the vinyl covering sheathing the cable, a surface that felt as if it were coated with grease. The lubricant oozed, collecting in front of her legs, her arms, her hands, even her forehead, as she tried to pull herself ever more snugly against the lifeline.

"Wheeler!" she shrieked as the momentum of her descent increased and terror blossomed beyond her ability to think.

Her feet thudded on a solid surface.

"The elevator car," she gasped. But before she could process the good result, that surface gave way under the weight of her body on the elevator car's Plexiglas ceiling. The transparent sheet bowed, then snapped and popped just before it gave.

Again MaryBeth scrambled, clawing for any hand hold. Framework supports crackled then exploded like thunder in the enclosure. Kicking and screaming, MaryBeth plummeted, then plopped as she sat rudely on her tush. The landing left her sprawled, arms and legs akimbo surrounded by shards of broken plastic ceiling on the floor of the empty elevator car.

Looking around, she gingerly moved arms and legs, trying, at the same time, to get her bearings. She thanked God first, that she did not seem to be seriously injured. Secondly, she was terribly grateful there were no people in the elevator car, no one to break her fall or any innocent person she might have crushed. Also on the plus side, there was no one present to witness her indignity. The elevator doors were closed, concealing her from eyes in the hoped-for corridor outside.

She sat sprawled there a long moment catching her breath and trying to visualize and review what had happened.

The hands that had grabbed her shoulders were small but very firm. The arms must have been strong to have heaved her forward into the elevator shaft with such authority. No, rethinking, she decided it wasn't strong arms that prodded, it was a body...a short, soft but firm, substantial body. Man or woman? She didn't know.

Moving her arms and legs, rolling ankles and wrists to assure there was no significant injury, MaryBeth reached for the handrail that bordered the car about waist-high. Her feet slipped and shimmied and her ankles wobbled as she struggled to lift herself upright. Brushing her clothing, she peered down, assessing the damage.

Black and gray grease covered her hands and arms and legs and left a distinct streak up and down the middle of her wadded dress that was hiked up, barely covering what her grandparents had referred to as "her privates."

Her hands shook as she clamped them firmly about the metal railing, steadying herself as she took stock. For the moment she needed to establish in her mind what had just happened, then move beyond that to what action needed to come next. She needed to reconnoiter, to breathe deeply, straighten her clothes and her attitude, and recover her sense of propriety. She tugged at the hem of her dress, pulling, arranging it to cover her grease-smeared thighs.

The elevator lurched and what was left of MaryBeth's manicured fingernails bent backward as she dug her fingers into the metal railing. The elevator descended at a slow, reasonable speed, then stopped. The bell dinged, the doors opened, and MaryBeth ended her terrifying ride staring directly into the concerned frowns of Gray Wheeler and Lieutenant Pepper Butz. Their expressions became bewilderment, jarring her out of her shock as the looks on their faces ran a course from surprise to concern, to curiosity, to alarm.

Heroically, MaryBeth attempted a smile. She brushed grease-smudged hands over her skirt, an effort to reassure she was properly covered and tidied, a ridiculous gesture given her condition.

As if in lock step, the two men studied the broken Plexiglas on the car's floor, raised their faces to regard the ragged hole in the elevator's ceiling, and lowered their gazes back to MaryBeth, speechless, apparently waiting for an explanation.

"We heard you scream," Wheeler said at last. "What were you doing in there?"

"You imbecile. What do you think I was doing?" She glowered at him in disbelief as she stepped out of the elevator with all the dignity she could muster. She hobbled slightly as she passed between the two men.

Butz and Wheeler exchanged puzzled glances.

"I know this guess is probably wrong, but it looks like you've been mud wrestling." Wheeler shook his head looking mystified.

She didn't dignify the guess with a response or even a glance.

Butz answered Wheeler's shrug with one of his own and both men started after her, trailing at a respectful distance.

She stopped at the building's exit. Hanging onto the door handle with both hands, she froze for a moment before she began to shake.

"I was almost killed," she muttered quietly toward the closed door as her two companions caught up.

Wheeler grabbed her arm. "In an elevator? Alone? How? What happened?"

She shrugged, pulling her arm from his grasp, and examined the scrapes and scratches, surprised that they were not gashes. "I need a minute."

Gray stared at the grease on his hand, rubbed his palms together, then wiped them both on his jacket. Butz stepped to her other side. "Did Simonovsky say something?"

"Did he do something?" Wheeler said, his voice a threatening growl.

"No. I sneaked out of the library without telling

him." She turned to face them. "The elevator doors were standing wide open. I thought how lucky that was, and I hoped they would stay open a minute to help with my quick getaway. I looked back to see if Larry was following, if he had noticed yet that I was gone. So, I was looking behind me when I reached the elevator. When I got there, the car wasn't. I almost stepped into the empty elevator shaft. I grabbed the sides. Caught myself just in time. Then someone grabbed my shoulders from behind."

"Who?" the men chorused.

"…and shoved. The person pushed me into the empty shaft." Suddenly spent, she leaned against the heavy glass door that blocked her path to the sidewalk outside.

"Who would do something like that?" Gray demanded.

"I don't think I'm cut out for detective work." Her voice quivered, and she turned around to regard him plaintively.

Butz cleared his throat and spoke in an official tone. "Ms. Gilland, can you identify the person or persons who pushed you into an open elevator shaft?"

Whimpering, MaryBeth inhaled and stood straighter without taking her eyes from Wheeler's face. She bit her bottom lip, then shifted her gaze to Butz.

"No. I didn't see him at all. His hands gripping my shoulders felt small, but thick. They were also smooth. Almost feminine." She shivered and shook her head, appealing to Wheeler for understanding. "It gives me the willies just to think of his little hands."

She hesitated. When no one else spoke, she continued with no prodding.

"And he smelled peculiar. He wore a fruity sweet cologne. It was grotesque. It wasn't something a normal man would wear at all. And he hunkered down. He shoved with his body, maybe his hip, and his hands at the same time. He hit me low. It buckled my knees, and I flew into the open shaft. It was like a nightmare."

"The person who pushed you into an open elevator shaft," Butz said, "was it Sprat?"

She shook her head and rolled her eyes. "I didn't see him. I couldn't identify him at all. I can't swear to anything."

"Could it have been Sprat?"

"I can't even give you a definite yes or no about whether it might have been him." Again, she hesitated before exhaling with a wheeze. "It could have been. It must have been, mustn't it? Unless... It probably had to be, didn't it, with those small, thick hands? Yes, I guess it probably was."

"Who else were you thinking of when you said, 'Unless?'" he asked.

"I was wondering about the nephew. That Wayne Tessler you mentioned."

"What about him?"

"Well"—she gave Gray a warning glance—"you don't happen to know if he's a tall man, do you? Or short?" She hesitated. "Maybe a short, round guy with unusually small hands?"

"No, I don't." The lieutenant looked at her as if he were concerned that the strain might have damaged her more than physically; like she might be having a nervous breakdown.

Tugging the cell phone out of his pants pocket, he scanned the lobby. Spying the telephone carrels, he hurried down the hall to position himself in one.

Still standing there, staring at MaryBeth, Gray opened his arms, inviting her to step closer.

With no hesitation, socialite/model MaryBeth Gilland, covered with grease, shoes and clothing in shambles, golden hair stringy with flyaway strands pointing several directions, eased into Gray Wheeler's arms making weird guttural noises in her throat.

Holding her, Gray raised his eyebrows and smiled at nothing in particular. Then his eyes rolled, the flexible brows veed to the bridge of his nose and the smile withered.

MaryBeth shuddered a sigh and tightened her arms around his waist, re-igniting his smile.

Chapter Thirteen
Police

Wheeler thumbed through magazines as he sat—elbows braced on his knees, both feet flat on the floor—at the edge of a rose-figured sofa in the posh living room of MaryBeth Gilland's apartment.

Pages flipped. He didn't have much interest in the periodicals' contents: beauty tips and tell-all stories of celebrities.

Forty minutes earlier, MaryBeth had disappeared into her bedroom assuring him she would "be right back."

Eventually, Gray heard the faint sound of the shower and afterward a hair dryer. There had been no sounds at all for the past several minutes. Gray glanced at the bedroom door occasionally, as he continued flipping pages on yet another glamour magazine. Scowling, still studying the door, he tossed the fanzine onto the glass sofa table in front of him and turned his frown to the mute, cordless telephone he had placed on the table to have it within easy reach.

He wanted Butz to call. He wanted to hear that police had arrested Sprat, needed assurance that there'd be no more life-threatening surprises on the person of MaryBeth Gilland. Eventually he slouched, rocked his head back against the pillowed cushions, clasped his hands over his belt buckle, and frowned at the ceiling.

He sat like that in the silence, flexing jaw muscles and biceps and thinking. Her first outing and they had come up against your basic, alpha-male-type murderer. He hadn't seen a case like this one in years. Why did it have to be both unusual and threatening? It had looked so simple—open and shut. This Sprat character was turning out to be damned imaginative, if he was responsible for uxoricide—a new word learned since Gray had begun investigations, and a new twist in an age-old question: how does a man rid himself of a rich wife and walk away free, with no one noticing? It was exhilarating, when you thought about it. Getting away with murder, winding up rich, and going scot-free.

He started when the telephone rang, causing him to leap to his feet and bolt from a comfortable slouch to rigidly upright. He answered before the first ring stopped echoing.

"Hello… Yeah, Butz, I've been waiting. Have you got him?" He listened a moment. "What?"

The bedroom door opened and MaryBeth stepped into the room. She wore low-rider slacks and an oversized sweater that draped provocatively covering her upper body only to stop abruptly, leaving her waist and the hollow hinting at her belly button exposed.

Wheeler raised his eyebrows but continued listening to Butz. After a pause, he shook his head in disbelief.

"I thought it was peculiar too. I figured he was following her and got a little heavy-handed when he saw the open elevator, an opportunity too good to pass up. Where do we go from here?" Another pause. "I'll ask her and get back to you. No, we'll take it easy. I sure never figured on this."

Wheeler set the cordless phone in its stand and paced three steps, feeling bewildered.

"The police picked Sprat up before noon on an old traffic warrant," he said quietly, standing still and gazing at MaryBeth. "They wanted to talk to him about the thing with his wife, so they wooled him around a little, dogging the paper work. He was there until after two-thirty."

MaryBeth returned his stare. "Then who…? I don't understand. If it wasn't Sprat, who pushed me into the elevator shaft? Why would a perfect stranger do that?"

"I don't know, but I'm pretty sure your assailant was no stranger, perfect or otherwise." Wheeler slumped back onto the sofa, let his arms hang limply at his sides and scowled down at his shoes. "I have to think this through again." He stared at his shoes for a long time.

MaryBeth remained standing, scarcely breathing.

"There isn't anyone who would want to injure you for any other reason, is there?" Wheeler asked. "Jealous models? Business associates?"

"Not a soul. I didn't have an enemy in the world…until I met you."

"What does that mean?" He stiffened and sat straighter to challenge her with a grim look.

"Nothing. I didn't really mean to suggest anything."

He waved a hand, letting it pass. "What do you need to do to finish getting ready?"

"I need to flip a curling iron through my hair. Go where?"

"To have a talk with Leland Jack Sprat."

"Known, before 2006, as Howard Kluz."

"Is that something Simonovsky came up with?"

"Yes."

"Why didn't you tell me before?"

"My thoughts have been otherwise occupied."

He nodded. "Okay, how long is this hair thing going to take?"

"Ten minutes, tops." She turned and hurried back through the bedroom door leaving it ajar.

Wheeler followed, deep in thought, but stopped at the doorjamb. He retreated a step as the whir of the hair dryer brought him up short. MaryBeth sat at a vanity, combing her hair with the fingers of one hand and aiming the nozzle of the hair dryer with the other.

He raised his voice to be heard over the dryer's hum. "Do you think you can face Sprat/Kluz and his tiny hands now that it turns out his may not be the hands of your nightmares?"

She regarded his reflection in the mirror. "Yes, because I'm more curious now than scared. I think we may need to get a look at this nephew of Treena and Clover's, Wayne Tessler. Also, I have a new policy. From now on, I'm doing all my investigating with you."

"I was right there when you went to the morgue."

"You weren't close enough. Because of the distance, I almost went directly from one morgue to the other."

Smirking at her in the mirror, Wheeler eased into the bedroom and walked over to stand behind her. "Starting to come around. Liking me better all the time, aren't you?"

She turned the nozzle on him. "That's too close," she snapped. "Haven't you ever heard of moderation?"

She turned off the hair dryer before he answered.

"I like excesses. Hot or cold. Rich or poor. Black or white. Moderation isn't stimulating."

"I'm a moderate person," she said, still speaking to his reflection. She grabbed a curling iron and flipped it through her long, blonde tresses.

He regarded her image in the mirror thoughtfully and nodded. "You may be the exception to my theory. Back to the review."

She continued combing her fingers through her hair and repositioning the iron. "If Sprat didn't push me into that elevator shaft, who did? Could it have been Wayne Tessler?"

Gray pivoted and paced to the door, pondering her question. They might need to take a serious look at the possibly nefarious nephew. "I guess so. I guess we need to find out if there are any other men in this caper with small hands."

MaryBeth squinted as if waiting for him to share her thought. "Right now, there are no other men in this caper, ones that we know of, anyway, with small hands or not. I would have noticed. I always notice that."

"Yeah," Gray muttered, still frowning. "Maybe Sprat can shed a little light on this. Come on. You look fine. Let's call Butz and meet him at Tessler's place."

"I look fine? What the heck is that supposed to mean?" She snapped the curling iron off.

"It means you look better than last night, but not as good as yesterday morning. Okay? It might be better if you didn't attract too much attention for a while anyway."

She looked steadily at his face. When he noticed, appreciation filled him with a sudden, self-conscious buoyancy. Apparently satisfied with the look, she returned his giddy grin with a moderate one.

"Fine is good enough for now, I suppose." She stood, stepped into her shoes, and followed him out.

****

Opening his apartment door, Treena and Clover's nephew Wayne Tessler stood sturdy six-feet tall, heavy through the hips and legs, his torso shaped like a pear. He wore an aged bathrobe over street clothes, even late in the afternoon.

Pale, his pudgy face was doughy. He had a sweet countenance and looked mildly interested as Gray introduced himself, then MaryBeth and Lieutenant Butz, who had caught up with them at the nephew's apartment door. Wheeler explained that he and his associate, assisting the police, were interviewing relatives of Clover Sprat, who was currently lying comatose at Mercy Hospital. He asked if Tessler had a few minutes to help them. The man stuffed his hands deeper into the pockets of his robe, turned without saying anything, and led them into his apartment without issuing an invitation. No one bothered to close the door.

The only thing threatening about Tessler, besides his size, as far as MaryBeth could see, was the glower, which lightened a little when his gaze shifted from Gray and Butz to her. His eyes scanned her, then he did a double-take and lost the slump, swelling maybe to six-foot-one, elongating the pear shape.

"I suppose you people are on their side, too," he said, setting angry eyes back on Gray. Addressing his annoyance at Wheeler, it appeared he didn't want to antagonize the woman or the cop.

Butz shook his head, mutely responding to the comment, but didn't speak. His silence made him appear neutral.

Gray grimaced and looked at the floor as if feeling guilty. It was rare to see the detective forego a smart-mouthed comeback. MaryBeth took a step closer to the nephew.

"Mr. Tessler, Treena hired my employer, Your Eyes Only Detective agency, to investigate Clover's situation. She was suspicious about Clover's unusual weight gain."

"I'll just bet she was. Eager to call for an investigation, too, as soon as her own ducks were in a row." His words sounded angry, but his expression softened again as his eyes engaged hers. He studied her a moment, then shrugged and lost more of the attitude. "Lucky for me she's got the mean reds for that cartoon character, Sprat. Bet she pointed every fat, bejeweled finger at the poor schmuck. She did accuse him of doing something dastardly, didn't she? She probably told you Clover was the victim of some foul deed and told you exactly who had done the deed, just needed you to figure a way to prove it. Isn't that right?" He sounded angry, but he looked as if he were pleading, not only with MaryBeth, but anyone else within earshot.

"Clover's your aunt. Aren't you concerned that she might be dying?" MaryBeth asked.

His attitude appeared to soften again. "Probably I'm genuinely more concerned about her than Treena is, but, no, I'm not involved. Neither of those women has ever had much to do with me."

"I thought Clover paid your way through college."

Butz and Wheeler were leaving MaryBeth the interview.

"Conscience money. Community college for two years, then an insignificant state school. Nothing to brag about. Tuition, books, essentials only."

"Did you have to work to help support yourself?"

"No, I didn't, but I wasn't able to pledge a fraternity either."

Wheeler cleared his throat. "How many years did you attend college?"

"You already checked, didn't you?"

Wheeler nodded.

"Okay, smart ass, I stayed in as long as the money held out. Clover was either too rich or too damn dumb to notice, so I kept enrolling. I had an associate's degree after two years at the community college. Four years at Southwestern. Six years, total."

"What do you do for a living now?" MaryBeth interrupted.

"I'm between jobs right now. I just moved here."

Lieutenant Butz muttered something, drawing all eyes toward him.

"What?" Wheeler asked.

"He's been here nearly three months," the lieutenant said.

"I've looked for work," Tessler defended. "Haven't been able to find anything."

"There are Help Wanted signs out all over town," Butz said.

"Sure, there are jobs if you're willing to pearl dive or flip burgers. I'm looking for something better than that. Something in my field. I'm qualified to work in a lot better jobs than what you're thinking."

MaryBeth stepped into the circle of men, all frowning at each other. "What is your degree in, Mr. Tessler?"

"You can call me Wayne."

"Okay. What is your field of expertise, Wayne?"

"Political science. I plan to run for elective office."

"Until then, what?"

"Work on someone else's campaign."

"Whose?"

"Haven't decided who I want to support yet."

"So, what have you been doing in the meantime?"

"Getting settled. Checking the lay of the land."

"Have you talked to your aunts?"

"What for?"

"To let them know you're in town. See if they have any connections; lines on any work you might do for potential political candidates who might need a well-educated guy like you."

"Didn't think of that." His puzzled frown mirrored hers. "Guess that might be an idea."

"So you haven't seen either Treena or Clover since you've been in town?"

"I didn't say that."

"Then you *have* seen them?"

"One of them."

"Which one?"

"Treena."

"Did you contact her, or did she reach out to you?"

"How could she have? How could she have known I was here?"

Wheeler obviously didn't like the cat and mouse game the guy was playing, dodging easy questions by coming back with questions of his own. "Come on,

Tessler. Cooperate. We're going to find out anyway. You might as well tell us. Are you in on some plan to murder Clover Sprat?"

"No."

"Did Treena Flowers bring you back here?"

"What do you mean?"

"Did she pay you to move back to the city?"

He looked away, then back at his interrogator. "She did."

"Why did she do that?"

"I guess she wanted me close. I am family, you know."

"Did she explain her sudden interest in your proximity?"

"No, and, to tell you the truth, I didn't ask."

Wheeler shot a look at MaryBeth to see if she had noticed the telltale disclaimer—*to tell you the truth*—the one she was sensitive to. She had.

"So you moved back to town but didn't contact the family member who summoned you?" Gray asked.

"I was already planning a move. This was as good a place as anywhere else."

"Why didn't you contact her after you arrived?"

"I already knew what she wanted. She told me before I came. She wanted me to help break up the Sprats' romance. By the time I got here, it was already too late. I trailed around after Clover and Sprat for a while, long enough to know they were a done deal. Treena threw a wad of cash at me and made a list of things she wanted me to do."

"Did you do them?" Wheeler asked.

"Hell, no. Her mistake. She shouldn't have paid for the work until it was done. That's a firm rule of mine.

You hand me the money, I'm done."

"Do you still have the list she gave you?"

"No. No evidence on the premises. You'll have to look somewhere else."

Butz perked up at the challenge. "How about if we get a search warrant?"

"You've got nothing to base a search warrant on. Legal studies were among my many electives, Lieutenant. No judge is going to let you paw through my home and my possessions without a valid reason, and you don't have one."

Butz pursed his lips as if considering Tessler's point, then lowered his eyes, yielding the argument.

"Will you tell us what was on the list?" MaryBeth's voice was conciliatory.

Wayne Tessler smiled for the first time since the visitors had come through the door of his apartment. "No," he rasped. "I won't even tell the lovely Ms. Gilland."

"Will you at least promise me that you didn't do any of the things on the list?"

His smiled broadened. "No. I wouldn't want to lie to you. I did carry out one of the requests, which I regret wholeheartedly, at this moment. If I had seen your face before, I never would have done it."

"Did you intend to do me serious injury?" The words were nearly a whisper. At the same moment, she lowered her gaze to his hands. They were both still concealed deep in the pockets of his robe.

"You figure it out, Ms. Detective. You seem to be pretty good at detecting."

"Will you confirm that I guessed correctly?"

"I will not. Not ever."

Chapter Fourteen
Rooming House

Following a brief meeting in the parking lot, the sleuths—the amateur and both professionals—parted company as they left Tessler's neighborhood. All three had reached the same conclusion: Wayne Tessler's hands—supposedly small but which none of them had seen—had shoved MaryBeth Gilland into the elevator shaft. On meeting her face to face, he regretted having done it. The move against her was presumably the first on Treena Flowers' list of jobs assigned to him. In light of his obvious regard, the investigators assumed Tessler would not make any further malicious attempts on MaryBeth's person, in spite of his refusal to confess he had done that initial odious thing.

Lieutenant Butz returned to his neglected duties at police headquarters.

Preoccupied, Wheeler drove as if he were alone.

MaryBeth shifted in her seat and started to speak twice, glanced at his stony countenance and held her silence.

"Eleven-four-ninety-four?" he asked quietly, staring sullenly at buildings they passed.

"What?"

He glanced at her. "Sprat's old address? Is it one-one-four-nine-four Constitution?"

"Yes." She hadn't imagined he would remember

such an obscure detail. On the other hand, she was usually good at remembering numbers, and the address sounded familiar. "I'm almost sure that's right."

"It's on the way. Let's take a look while we're in the neighborhood."

MaryBeth nodded without speaking and assumed he caught the nod out of the corner of his eye, because he didn't turn his head or acknowledge her agreement.

A mile or so later, Wheeler began squinting at house numbers. He pulled to the curb in front of a three-story frame house in the modest old neighborhood. A "Room for Rent" sign leaned in a front window.

He glanced at MaryBeth. Without exchanging a word, they got out of the car and strolled up the sidewalk toward the house, moving as if they both knew the plan.

Four broad concrete steps led onto a wide wooden porch whose aged planks groaned under their feet. The front door stood open behind a screen door. Wheeler pressed the doorbell which sounded, then echoed somewhere back in the far reaches of the house. They waited.

Eventually they heard footsteps and a stocky woman appeared, wiping her hands on a tea-towel as she waddled through the living room and to the open doorway.

She gave them a good-natured smile. "Hello. What can I do for you folks?"

Wheeler cleared his throat. "Good afternoon, ma'am. My name is Gray Wheeler, and this is MaryBeth Gilland. We are hoping you can give us some information about a fellow who used to be one of your boarders."

The woman nodded agreeably and pushed the screen door open to encourage them inside. "I'm Mrs. Goodner. Come in and let's see if I can help you."

As they stepped through the opened doorway, MaryBeth squeezed closer to Wheeler and whispered. "I thought you would come up with some elaborate cover story."

"Why?"

"That's the way they do it in the movies."

"The truth's easier. I usually just go with that unless there are extenuating circumstances."

"I'll try to remember that." MaryBeth scanned the high-ceilinged living room, smiled slightly at the faded rose wallpaper, and wondered at the collection of smells, coffee, tobacco smoke, food, humanity. Suddenly she caught the aroma of fresh yeast bread baking and her mouth watered as Mrs. Goodner led them through a dining room containing a long, trestle-type table with a dozen or more chairs, and into a large kitchen, obviously the source of most of the food smells wafting through the other rooms.

Mrs. Goodner motioned them toward chairs at an enamel-topped wooden kitchen table. "Could you use a cup of coffee?"

"No, thank you." MaryBeth sat and looked around, apprehensive enough about the coming conversation without adding caffeine.

"Yes." Gray eased into a chair at the head of the table. "I'd like a cup, if you don't mind."

The older woman smiled her approval.

"Mrs. Goodner, do you remember a man who lived here back in 2005 or 2006?" Wheeler began. "His name was either Howard Kluz or Leland Jack Sprat.

Mrs. Goodner shuffled efficiently across the gleaming linoleum floor to the stove, poured a mug of coffee, and returned to place it on the table in front of him.

"Sugar?" she said. "Or milk? I'm out of cream."

Wheeler shook his head and smiled as he sipped. Seeming satisfied, she nodded. "Certainly, I do...remember him, that is." She stood there looking docile enough, but spoke in an almost scolding tone which MaryBeth interpreted as annoyance that Gray might have implied she was addled. "He used both names for a time, don't you know, while he was making the changeover."

MaryBeth gave Gray a look of complete surprise.

He pretended to ignore her and took a long, noisy sip of his brew before he continued. "Great coffee."

"Thanks."

"Can you tell us what Mr. Sprat did for a living at that time?" He leaned back in the chair, fingering the cup handle, looking comfortable and not at all concerned about their hostess's answers. Trying to follow his lead, MaryBeth relaxed the ramrod stiffness in her back. It felt good.

"Which one?" Mrs. Goodner asked, pouring herself a cup. Instead of joining them at the table, she settled in a rocking chair near the stove. "Kluz or Sprat?"

"You mean they...ah...had different jobs?" MaryBeth blurted.

Gray gave her a warning look, but Mrs. Goodner was spooning sugar from a nearby canister into her cup and missed the exchange.

"Yes," she said agreeably. "Kluz sold life

insurance, don't you know. At the same time, he worked for that National Tax Service part time. With all of that heaped on him, he still took any odd jobs that came along."

MaryBeth slouched against the back of the chair. "He certainly sounds energetic."

"Oh, he was. The boy was never idle, not for one single minute, always improving himself, don't you know. He went to the library regular, checked out all kinds of books, mostly those that show a person how to do a thing. He put it all to good use, too, helping out around here, rewiring old lamps or fixing the plumbing or tilling my flower beds or something. And every evening he'd sit with his nose in those men's clothing catalogues." She paused for a sip of coffee before she added, "Or the occasional magazine."

"What kind of magazines?" Wheeler asked. "Newsweek or Time?"

"No, no. Not those magazines. Ones like Vogue and Glamour."

Without saying anything, Wheeler drank more coffee, waiting for Mrs. Goodner to fill the ensuing silence, which, as a congenial hostess, she did.

"He lifted weights regular, too, several times a day," she said, sounding proud. "He had them in his room at first, don't you know, but I had to ask him to move them down to the basement finally because he got to lifting real heavy ones and I was afraid they'd drop right through the floor.

"Of course, he took classes nights."

"What kind of classes?" Wheeler asked, taking another appreciative sip of his coffee, pretending he wasn't hypnotized by every word, that he didn't feel like they had hit the mother lode of information regarding the mysterious Jack Sprat.

"Well, first he tried mortician's school," the older woman said, "but he didn't take to that. Then he went off some place every Saturday to learn to drive an ambulance. Different times, he took typing classes and accounting classes and landscape design classes, and went to just about every kind of school you can imagine. He was particularly good at accounting. Seemed to have a real knack for it. That's how he got the job with that National Tax Service outfit."

"Did you know he planned to change his name?" Wheeler asked.

"Oh, sure. You see, he had been in some trouble when he was a youngster…"

"What kind of trouble?" Wheeler interrupted.

"I never did know, exactly. Never really wanted to know. It was police trouble back in Oklahoma or Illinois or where ever it was he was from. Anyway, it had caused him to break from his family when he was just a young scamp."

After several moments of sipping and compliments and indications he was savoring his coffee, Gray said, "How long did Jack live here with you, Mrs. Goodner?"

"Well, he came to me sometime in 2005, as I recall. I'm not exactly sure. I could look it up for you, if you like." She rocked forward as if getting to her feet, but Wheeler motioned her back.

"It's not important," he said.

"He had just split up with a girlfriend and he was pretty unhappy," she continued, leaning to toe the floor and push her rocking chair a couple of times. "But he wasn't the kind to sit and mope, don't you know. Less than a week after he started staying here, he got out and got a job and began going to night schools. He never worked just one job either. He always had two or three at the same time."

"I suppose he made a lot of money, then?" Gray said.

"It's likely he did." As the rocker slowed, she sipped her coffee.

"What did he spend his money on?"

"I don't know. He rode the bus. Didn't have a car for the longest time. He lived real careful. He was what you might call 'tight' with his money. I can't say as I know how he spent it, if he did. He wasn't the type to squander. He paid his rent on time, though sometimes I had to remind him. A couple of times, I reminded him twice."

"Do you remember when he changed his name?"

"Sure do. It was not a year later. I baked him a red velvet cake—which was his favorite—and we had a bit of a celebration. He thought about the change for a long time. He planned it to coordinate with changing jobs and all. When everything was ready, he went down to that social security office and applied for a new number to go with his new name."

"Did he tell them he wanted a second number?"

"I don't know whether he did, or not. Why would he? I think he just got a new name and a new number. Then, he borrowed my car, took the driving test, showed those people his new Social Security, and got a new driver's license under his new name.

"That same week he started a new job, and he enrolled in one of those spa places where they train for bodybuilding competition, don't you know. That's when he started driving the ambulance. Also, that's about the time he moved. I sure hated to lose him. He was wonderful to have around, so handy to fix things and all."

"Did you lose track of him after that?" MaryBeth asked, forcing the words around a frog in her throat. Mrs. Goodner sounded genuinely fond of Sprat. From her description, he sounded like an ambitious, energetic, kind man. How could such a fellow calculate and follow through with the murders of older, vulnerable women?

"Good lands, no," Mrs. Goodner said. "He got all set up in a little apartment of his own. I worried about him. I didn't even know if he could cook or not. I'd done his ironing for him, as well as cooking for him. Turned out, he had started chef classes, and he began practicing. Soon as I knew, I gave him some of my old pots and pans and utensils, don't you know.

"Right at first, he would stop by at supper time and eat with me and whoever all was staying here. When he got more used to being alone, he'd give me a call now and again, sometimes just to say hello and sometimes wanting one of my recipes. It was kind of funny, exchanging recipes with Howard…er…Leland…or…it was Jack he asked me to call him at last. Never mind that. Of course, he invited me to his wedding."

Gray appeared both fascinated and mystified. "Which wedding was that?"

"When he married the Swenson woman. I didn't go, of course, not thinking that was any of my business, so to speak."

MaryBeth sat up straighter, suddenly alert again.

Distracted by her abrupt movement, Gray gave her

an admiring glance, approving her enthusiasm and encouraging her to put in a question here and there.

"Were you happy for him?" MaryBeth asked.

Mrs. Goodner shifted in her chair and grimaced, apparently not wanting to make any unkind judgments. "Well...she was older," she began. "Much older. They said she was attractive, of course, but not at all the kind of female you would expect could hold onto a ball of fire like our Jack. She was obviously rich, and Jack had come from nothing, of course."

"Who told you that, do you remember?"

"About her being rich?"

"Yes." Again Mrs. Goodner shifted, frowning at nothing in particular for a moment. "Certainly I do. Of course. Nothing wrong with my mind. It was Sadie." Mrs. Goodner looked surprised at their reactions before adding, "I don't suppose you know about Jack and Sadie. There's really no reason you should."

Neither of her guests spoke, their silence prodding her to continue.

"Sadie Olivia was one of my boarders. Lived here for maybe half a year, don't you know, some of it during the same time Jack was here.

"She's a pretty thing, our Sadie. Bound and determined to get into acting. Twenty-four is maybe a little old to be starting an acting career, but she was game. Changed her last name from Brown or Smith or something common to Olivia hoping to help her get started. She did actually get her first career job while she was living here. Even when she did, it wasn't for acting, though. She got a modeling gig.

"Sadie and Jack talked together quite a bit. They got close. They had so much in common, all that youthful energy and beautiful bodies. Also they were terribly ambitious. Both of them."

"Were they lovers?"

Mrs. Goodner smiled. "Yes. I know for fact that Sadie fell hard. I don't know if Jack even knew it at first, or if he just ignored her feelings. I got the idea he thought they were enjoying each other casually, fulfilling their mutual needs without the bother of a commitment, don't you know?

"When their friendship reached a certain point, she said something about living together or marriage or an agreed arrangement of some kind. She told me she planned to talk to him about it. After that, she sulled up for quite a while. Finally told me, woman-to-woman, she thought Jack might be peculiar, don't you know, the kind of man who doesn't like females exclusively. She was awfully discouraged, but I'll tell you one thing, there is no quit in Sadie. She lightened up and began chasing Jack as doggedly as she chased her career. Never has given up, as far as I know, right up to this very day, even after she accepted in her mind how money hungry he was. She understood he didn't intend to let himself get saddled by someone just because she appealed to him physically. She said he was sick to death of being poor. He planned to end his close relationship with poverty as quick as he could. Said he was determined to try rich for a change. Money, of course, was the one thing Sadie couldn't give him.

"I think she didn't give up the pursuit because she knew she had a hold on him. He craved her. Of course, he is thirty-six years old now and a handsome devil, but getting on up in years. The attention of a looker like Sadie probably flattered him."

Mrs. Goodner suddenly gave MaryBeth a harsh look. "You know, now that I think about it, Sadie bears a strong likeness to you, Ms. Gilland. You aren't related to her, are you?"

"No, ma'am," MaryBeth said, but she shot a quick look at Gray. He gave a little nod indicating he, too, remembered the young woman Sprat had met for dinner.

MaryBeth said, "Mrs. Goodner, I'm going to ask you a very important question. You've mentioned that Howard or Leland or Jack has an unusual regard for money."

The older woman nodded.

"Do you think Howard Kluz or Leland Jack Sprat is obsessive enough about money to commit murder to get it?"

Mrs. Goodner's face twisted into a resistant frown and she withdrew physically, pressing back into the rocking chair. She shook her head slightly and pulled her coffee cup protectively close to her chest.

"You're asking if he might have killed Mrs. Swenson...that is, Mrs. Sprat." She shook her head from side to side slowly indicating the answer was no, but she didn't say it. Finally, she spoke.

"I don't believe so. Jack's a kindly sort, in spite of his rugged good looks and manly ways. I can't feature him doing anything violent to any other human being, even for bags of money."

Chuffing and shrugging, Mrs. Goodner rocked forward, rose rather haughtily and paced to the sink. MaryBeth and Gray glanced at one another but when neither spoke, the older woman added, "Jack was never one for violence." She placed her cup in the sink, then strode to the dining room door. MaryBeth thought the landlady was going to invite them to leave, but that was before she spoke again.

"That is to say..." She hesitated and it looked as if she were working through some thought process. "Who knows what even a kind, easy-going person might do in the throes of a walleyed, hissy fit?"

"Does Jack have fits of temper?" MaryBeth asked quietly.

Mrs. Goodner gazed for a moment at the dishwater, then shook her head as if rejecting a thought. "No. For the most part, he is a calm, cool, gentle man. But...when an easy-going person loses his temper...well, he can surprise you. I'd call them tantrums. Unreasonable anger. Like a little kid might throw."

"Did you yourself ever see him lose his temper?" MaryBeth asked.

"I saw him get pretty upset a couple of times with Sadie, but I never saw him act like he cared that strongly about anyone else. I don't believe his marriage ran to violence or great passion in any direction, don't you know?"

Gray nodded as Mrs. Goodner turned to look at him.

"He would be more a man who would plan something and devise behavior to go with it?" Gray suggested.

"Yes," the landlady brightened. "Whenever he has a project, Jack follows a plan. I watched him plan a dozen different projects. He stuck with every one all the way to the end. He went in for detail, drew diagrams, sometimes cut little pictures out of newspapers or magazines. I cleaned his room regular and I saw his projects on paper. I never once saw one for murder or a theft or a crime of any kind."

She looked to MaryBeth as if for a comment. "I'm sure if he did something terrible," the older woman continued, her gaze appealing to MaryBeth, "he would have had a plan. Everything he did he worked out in detail. The man never did anything spur of the moment. He is not what I would consider a spontaneous type of individual."

MaryBeth lowered her voice nearly to a whisper. "But you do think he might be capable of murder?"

The landlady clenched her teeth and fists and sobered again, shaking her head. "No. Not at all. What I'm saying is, I don't like to think so."

"But you do think he would be capable of murdering someone, don't you?"

The woman lowered her head and stared at the floor without answering.

"Mrs. Goodner," Gray's voice was mellow, compelling, "did you think it was odd when the first Mrs. Sprat died just a few months after she and Jack were married?"

Mrs. Goodner remained standing, but her shoulders slumped, as if fatigue had overtaken her. "Well, no, not at the time." She sounded both reluctant and evasive. "Like I said, she was an older woman. I never set eyes on her, personally, but I heard she was a full-figured woman, on the fleshy side. I supposed she knew she didn't have many years left and she married Howard…Leland…Jack to brighten her last days."

"Or hurry them along," Gray said under his breath. In a normal speaking voice he continued. "Did Jack inherit money from the first Mrs. Sprat?"

"I suppose he did. A little. I'd say maybe he earned it, however much it was. He came by to see if his old room was available, but I was full up at the time. He stayed with Sadie a while, but the situation with them was tense, so he left. I don't believe he would have come back here to live if he had inherited enough to get an apartment of his own. I'll tell you something else. He grieved for the woman. He pretty well went down in the dumps after she died."

She straightened, taking heart. "Jack could be a wonderful comfort to a woman. When he lived here, even when he was only here for that short time, he was always helping out around the place, eager to please. He might have had a mother fixation. He treated older women gently, tenderly, like we all were his mother.

"I've been close to most of the young people who've lived here with me. On the one hand, women want someone to stroke them, to pet them, and talk sweet to them. That's what women look for in a man, don't you know.

"It's been my experience that a man looks for a woman who'll feed him. I guess it's because they associate early love with the mother who feeds them and they never really get far beyond that.

"When they're living here, I feed them and they think of that as me loving them. Mostly they do what they can to show me they love me back."

MaryBeth spoke quietly. "Then, Mrs. Goodner, are you saying you think Jack Sprat might be inclined to show love by feeding someone?"

"Yes." Mrs. Goodner said, brightening. "That's just the kind of thing he might do. Like I said, he was always eager to do things to get approval."

A timer sounded. Mrs. Goodner turned and hurried through a door which obviously led to a utility room.

"MaryBeth," Gray said in a stage whisper, "you're talking yourself out of our only suspect in this case."

"Maybe we should try looking for another one," she said, puzzling over Mrs. Goodner's comments.

"Who?" he asked.

"If it isn't Jack, who has the most to gain by Clover Sprat's death, especially her death at this specific time?"

"I don't know. Who?"

"That's what I'm asking you," she said impatiently. "You're the experienced detective here. You can't expect me to do all the crime-solving myself."

"Sweetheart, in a homicide, anybody can come up with questions. That's not the tough part of detecting. The tough part is coming up with answers."

She looked surprised. "Okay, I've been doing the amateur's part, feeding you pertinent questions. Now you need to contribute something, don't you know," she finished, mimicking Mrs. Goodner. She stood and looked toward the utility room door, then raised her voice. "Thank you, Mrs. Goodner, for your help."

MaryBeth walked toward the utility room just as Mrs. Goodner reappeared. MaryBeth patted the older woman's shoulder. "Meeting you has been both pleasant and enlightening."

Mrs. Goodner walked to the sink and turned on the water to rinse the coffee cup she had left there earlier, then she linked arms with MaryBeth for a slow procession to the front door.

Though not invited to join them, Gray Wheeler

swigged the last of his coffee, took his cup to the sink, rinsed it, and followed the ladies out.

Mrs. Goodner was smiling into MaryBeth's face, a startling contrast of old and young. "It's been nice meeting you, too. By the way, I have a vacant room now, don't you know. If you hear of someone nice who needs a place, steer them my way."

"We will."

In the passenger seat, MaryBeth looked woeful as she turned to wave good-bye.

In an attempt to draw her back to the present, Gray said, "She didn't even recognize you. Does that bother you?"

"What are you asking, Wheeler? Do you think I should feel like a has-been?"

Gray winced. "You know perfectly well that wasn't what I meant."

MaryBeth wasn't in a mood for placating. "Yes, well, maybe I do feel a little over the crest of my modeling career, but then looking at you makes me feel better." She gave him a sidelong glance, and he braced himself. "I am consoled by the thought that it's better to be a has-been than a never-was."

Gray said a quiet, "Touché." At the same time, he made a mental note. Crossing verbal swords with MaryBeth Gilland could be hazardous to one's ego, although the damage was mitigated by the sparkle in her eyes and the hint of a smile just before she zinged him. This partnership was working out fine, just fine.

He risked a long, heated look at her. Yes, sir, this partnership had potential written all over it.

Chapter Fifteen
Options

"Okay." Gray frowned as MaryBeth buckled her seat belt and he started the car. "Let's go back to square one. Who, besides Sprat, has any motive to kill Clover? And why would that same who want to get rid of you?"

"Maybe the two attacks aren't even connected," she said, glancing behind before he pulled into traffic.

"You mean someone with small hands propped the elevator doors open with no car present thinking to chuck whoever came along into an elevator shaft and, coincidentally, that person was you?"

"Doesn't seem logical, does it?"

"No kidding. Now, let's make a list of who benefits from Clover's demise."

MaryBeth shrugged. "I guess it will be a pretty short list."

"Sprat obviously holds first place," Gray said, undeterred, "but he doesn't seem to want his wife to die. Next possibility is the nephew. He also doesn't seem interested in the demise of Clover Sprat. Sexy Sadie rambled through my mind for consideration, but her standing with Jack doesn't seem secure enough for her to take that kind of risk. So, what do you think?"

"What about Treena?"

"What? Our very own client?" Gray frowned at her for a long moment. "Does Treena have a motive?"

"Possibly disinherited by an impending change in Clover's will." MaryBeth returned his frown.

"She's the one who brought the idea that her sister's death might be a homicide to everyone's attention, so it can't be her. Can it?"

"I suppose not."

"Right. Probably not her." His voice dropped at the words, emphasizing the Probably. "Who else? Back to the doughboy? The nephew? The obscure son of Clover and Treena's deceased and all-but-forgotten sister. The guy who didn't inherit anything when his super rich grandfather died. Old what's-his-name might be angling for a cut, I suppose."

"His name's Wayne."

"Right."

"Tessler," MaryBeth said. "Let's don't make the mistake of forgetting him again."

"Wayne Tessler. Yes. I knew that." Not only was this woman easy on the eyes, she was bright as a penny. "As far as we know, he's the only other character in this caper who might possibly inherit from Clover."

At a traffic light, Mary Beth stared at Gray. "Caper?" She squinted at him in disbelief. "That sounds like something out of a 1940's movie."

He pointed at the light, which had turned green. "Let's concentrate on the question." His ego was not yet re-inflated enough to handle another self improvement lecture.

MaryBeth scowled out at the passing scenery. "There has to be someone else. If the killer is not the grieving husband or his girlfriend, the nephew, or our client, then who? Are we certain it can't be any of those?"

"Pretty sure."

"Tell me again, why did we eliminate Treena?"

"First off, because she probably inherited the same amount of their dad's money that Clover did. They are sisters. If she's rich, she doesn't need her sister's money or insurance or anything. Not needing Clover's money erases a big incentive." Gray liked the way that sounded. The argument made sense. So, he continued.

"Also, she's the one who called police attention to her sister's condition. In the third place, she's the one who's hired us to investigate her sister's…ah… situation."

"Ah, yes," MaryBeth agreed, "and what was it exactly that the woman hired us to do?"

Gray clenched his teeth at the painful thought process. "To prove Sprat killed—or was in the process of killing—Clover. She didn't ask us to discover someone who might be trying to whack good old Clover. No. She made it easy to adopt her assumption that the charming, young, handsome-but-impoverished husband had a traditional motive. After all, he obviously would be the heir to his wife's fortune."

"Frame job?"

"Doesn't seem likely."

They shared a thoughtful pause. "I've read that a murderer cannot benefit from his victim's death." MaryBeth said. "Have you ever heard of that?"

"Yes."

MaryBeth brightened. "Besides that, Treena didn't come to us first. First she went to the police for help, told them about what she perceived to be a plot in progress. Surely she wouldn't have called official attention to the deed if she were the perpetrator." She gave him a questioning look. "But she might have wanted to cast suspicion on the husband just in case he was named in Clover's will to inherit her entire estate."

"Plus, the weight gain made it look like he was pursuing a plan." Gray was getting into the theory.

"The scheme was so quirky that it got Butz's attention," MaryBeth said. "There's no doubt Jack made Clover fat."

"No disagreement there."

"Her condition certainly is a major factor in her impending demise."

"Right again."

"Was a baseball bat conveniently located within reach of the alleged perpetrator?"

"You are spot-on. He definitely aided and abetted in making her fat, and he does have access to a possible murder weapon, in this case the bat. It sounds like we've talked ourselves full circle right back to the individual we suspected in the first place."

"Right."

"So who would anybody naturally suspect?"

"Whom?" she said, correcting him with the question.

"What?"

"Whom would anybody naturally suspect?"

"I thought we had pretty well agreed on the most likely whom," he said, a little taken aback by the interruption. "Besides, I believe your correction is grammatically incorrect."

"Don't get me confused."

"Okay, you're right. Sprat definitely is consensus first choice as the heavy in the plot."

They were silent.

"Besides that, if he was at police headquarters when I was pushed into the elevator shaft…" MaryBeth's voice trailed off, but Gray picked up the thought.

"Who do you like as first runner-up in this saga, his faithful sidekick?"

"Saga?"

"Don't start that again. Your physical presence is distraction enough without throwing in linguistic corrections and challenging my words of art. I'm thinking out loud here."

"Realizing that effort—thinking—is a strain on your brain, I will refrain."

He did a double take and grinned. "Very poetic. Did you do that on purpose?"

"It's a gift," she said, waving her hand as if erasing the words from the air.

"To continue, Mrs. Flowers asked us to do more than satisfy her curiosity. She sweetened the deal, using money as a widely accepted incentive."

MaryBeth regarded Gray. "Do you think she thought 'Your Eyes Only' was a substandard agency bumbling along, focused entirely on its own money problems?"

It was Wheeler's turn to scowl. "The agency has never had any money problems. We pay our bills on time or, at least somebody does. Don't forget, we were not established as a profit-making outfit. We were set up strictly to do company stuff—background checks on new employees, dabble in a little industrial snooping. No, I don't think she came to me…us…because she thought we were incompetent."

"Okay." MaryBeth looked contrite. "I didn't mean

to impugn your integrity or hurt your feelings or anything, but you did light up when she offered the bonus if we could get enough proof to get Sprat charged."

"Sweetened by the bonus if there is evidence enough to bind him over for trial."

"What I'm wondering is if Mrs. Flowers has some other reason for wanting Sprat charged and convicted? Which brings us back to the question of how Clover was changing her will."

"What are you talking about now?"

"The codicil. The amendment to her will that is ready and waiting to be signed. I wonder who benefits from the change."

"We probably need to find out." He smiled.

"Do you think Sprat knows the answer?"

"Why don't we ask him?"

"What if he doesn't tell us the truth?"

"There's always that possibility."

"How will we know?"

"Look for twitches."

"Is this more of your detective expertise? What do you mean? What am I supposed to look for?"

"When someone's lying, often he will twitch. You know, a lip will curl or an eye will wink or he'll pop his knuckles. He'll twitch."

"Wheeler! Is that the kind of stuff they teach people in private eye school?"

"Were you or were you not skeptical at first about the ants?"

"Yes."

"And?"

She shrugged. "Okay, so you were right…once."

"Trust me about twitches. Watch for even the slightest movement. Of course, an accomplished liar, someone with years of practice, won't twitch much, but he probably won't look you straight in the eye either.

"I'm afraid I might laugh."

"What?"

"If Sprat starts twitching, snarling his lip, blinking his eyes, popping his knuckles, I'm afraid I'll get tickled."

"I admit it takes self discipline, a certain savoir faire, and a modicum of restraint to be a detective. Let's hope you have enough to get you by."

MaryBeth ventured a dubious glance as he gunned the engine, swung the car into a parking place on the street, and turned the key off. She collected her purse.

"Advice on maturity," she sighed, "from the man who brings us ants in the pants and lip curling twitches? I don't think so."

Chapter Sixteen
Collusion

Gray guided MaryBeth through the dingy hallway, threading through a collection of tired-looking police; frowzy, mumbling suspects; attorneys in wrinkled clothing and even more wrinkled expressions, and an odd assortment of unidentifiable persons.

He opened the door marked "Office" without knocking.

Three men—two stood, addressing one seated behind the desk—stopped their earnest discussion to turn angry eyes on the newcomers. The glares yielded quickly to Wheeler's as he cleared his throat, preparing to speak. His body language sent all three occupants out the door, as if satisfied with the excuse to surrender the dingy room to the new arrivals.

Gray motioned MaryBeth into a wooden chair located at one side of the desk. The oaken desk and three chairs looked as if they had seen better days. All the wooden furnishings were carved with initials as if they had done time locked in a room with idle hands and sharp objects.

Gray pulled a metal folding chair leaning against a wall over and popped it open to sit close beside MaryBeth. Neither of them spoke.

Gray stood as Lieutenant Butz led Leland Jack Sprat into the room. Sprat's hands were free. No cuffs.

Sprat did not look at either Gray or MaryBeth, simply stared at the floor, as if preoccupied with thoughts of his own, or maybe trying to appear grief-stricken.

Butz stepped behind the desk and assumed another ancient wooden chair, nodding Sprat into the only remaining seat in front of the desk.

"Mr. Sprat," Butz said, when they all were seated, "this is MaryBeth Gilland." He waved a hand in her direction. "And Gray Wheeler." He indicated the room's other occupant. "I've invited them to sit in on our conversation, if that's all right with you."

Sprat gave them each a cursory glance, then shrugged and nodded. He looked tired.

"Mr. Sprat," Butz intoned, "you do understand that you don't have to talk to me…er…to us at all. If it would make you feel more comfortable, we'll be glad to wait for you to call an attorney or a friend to keep you company here. Do you want to call anyone?"

"No, let's get this over with. I need to get back to the hospital. She might come around and be frightened. I want to be there if she wakes up."

Butz gave Gray a curious glance. "We realize you don't want to be away long. We'll try to get the information we need and get you back as quick as we can. We just have some questions about Mrs. Sprat's situation. I think we all appreciate her condition is critical at this point. If she lives, which we hope she does, she'll be able to answer these questions for us herself."

Sprat leaned forward with his head down, elbows braced on his knees, and stared at his hands, which hung limp between his legs.

MaryBeth wondered if he were trying to conceal any telltale jerks and twitches by keeping his head down. Then, studying him, she realized he was trying to conceal something else. Watching in disbelief, she witnessed the beginning of crocodile tears that puddled in his eyes, then spilled, tracking down the man's face before they dropped to the floor.

She looked at Gray who glanced toward her, answering her unspoken questions with a puzzled frown and a shrug. Butz remained silent.

The episode lasted only a few seconds, then Sprat wiped both his eyes with the palms of his hands and drew a deep, shuddering breath, but did not look up.

"To be honest with you, Lieutenant," Sprat began quietly, "Clover is the best thing that ever happened to me."

Butz nodded what looked like approval, but MaryBeth remembered her time-proven theory. It had been her experience that when someone said, "To make a long story short," it was usually too late. Similarly the words, "To be honest..." or "To tell you the truth," usually prefaced exactly the opposite.

Butz said, "Please, go on."

"In the months we've been married, I've told Clover everything—I mean every rotten, mean, petty thing about me. Do you know what?" Everyone else in the room remained mute. Sprat gave Butz a look that was a mixture of joy and puzzled amazement. "She loves me anyway.

"All my life I've been trash. Everyone's thrown me out: parents, relatives, foster parents, everyone. I didn't blame them. None of them even knew how bad I really was.

"Before we got married, I told Clover things to shock her. She didn't act shocked or even surprised. When that stuff didn't faze her, I told her more…and then more after that. Nothing shook her. Then I got down to the bottom of the barrel, so to speak. I told her the worst stuff of all. The criminal stuff. You know what she said? She said anyone would forgive the things I did, if they knew me. If they knew how much living so corrupt, so crooked, so filthy, bothered me. She wrapped her arms around me.

"I broke down right there and cried like a baby. No one had made me cry since I was eight years old." When he looked up, the tears had begun again. "Now, I bawl just thinking of her, just thinking I might be losing her. The woman knows everything about me. She is the only human being who knows what a complete phony I am, and she loves me in spite of it. Her love is the purest, sweetest thing I've ever known in my life. No one ever loved me after finding out half the stuff Clover knows. No one ever saw, much less loved, who I am, deep down in my heart.

"After telling her all that, I felt better. She said she hoped getting that garbage out would make me feel cleansed, like I could start all over again. Just her and me. Fresh."

With that, he covered his face with both hands. "I don't think I can live with her gone from this world." His voice broke and his shoulders shook as sobs racked his body.

Embarrassed to be witnessing such an intimate display, MaryBeth swallowed tears of her own and frowned at the floor.

Moments later, Gray dug down in his pants pocket

and handed the man a tissue. Sprat took it, but he continued bawling for several ticks before he blew his nose and coughed. He looked as if he were trying to rein in his runaway emotions.

When he raised his eyes, Sprat looked only at Butz. "I didn't deserve to be in her life. No way. Much less to be married to her. No, sir, no way. I've never known anyone as good as she is."

MaryBeth looked from Sprat to Butz to Wheeler. Neither of the faces of the men on her team reflected any emotion—not sympathy nor disapproval. Their expressions were blanks. And she noted that Sprat spoke of his wife in present tense, as if he had not come to terms with her departure, was not yet thinking of her as deceased.

Butz broke the silence first. "Mr. Sprat, let me ask a question here. If you appreciate Mrs. Sprat so much, why do you keep company with other women?"

Sprat's expression turned venomous as he raised his eyes to glower at Butz. "Because Clover wants me to. She insists I do it." He grimaced as if the admission were painful. "Just because I'm younger than her." He looked from Butz to Wheeler as if appealing to them as men to understand. "I have a strong sex drive. Clover makes love with me every time I want her. Lord knows I try to hold back, but it's like she's able to tell when I need...well, you know. It was her idea for me to get myself a girl—someone younger—on the side. She wants me to have everything I want all the time, and she tries to see to it that I do. I mean that's just the way she is."

"We know about Sadie."

Suddenly Sprat stole a first, quick glance at

MaryBeth, smiled slightly, and lowered his voice. "I'll tell you the gospel truth. Clover gets the full benefit of my time with Sadie. Every time I get out and get…well…refreshed, so to speak, I come home more eager than ever to take care of Clover, and wait on her, and be good to her. Can't you see how it is?" He looked back at Wheeler. "With her being so good to me like that, it makes me want to repay her any way I can.

"Do you know what she does?" His earnest stare made the other three people in the room shake their heads, not quite sure if they wanted to know, or not. He continued, anyway. "Every week she gives me five hundred dollars walking-around money. She's already given me every kind of credit card you can imagine, every one with my own name on it. She doesn't hold anything back. I'm telling you, she's the most generous rich person I've ever known."

MaryBeth supposed her face showed her confusion as Sprat finally settled his restless gaze on her. Butz and Wheeler, their eyes locked on Sprat, appeared to be listening with their ears and other senses, trying to glean the truth from his free-running words.

Another lengthy silence ended with Butz. "Since you've been married to her, Sprat, the woman must have gained a hundred pounds?"

Sprat's expression darkened and he rasped as he set an angry stare on the lieutenant. "So what? What about it?"

"Exactly. That's what I want to know. What about it?"

"Like I told you, she's good to me. I can't help being thoughtful of her right back. Clover loves to eat. She gets this genuine enjoyment—I'd say it's almost like sexual pleasure—out of food. Watching her, well, I've gotta say it looks like the sensation I get during an orgasm." He shot another quick look at MaryBeth. "What I mean to say is: being with a woman. Have they passed some law against people eating whatever they want whenever they want it?"

He paused, but when no one answered his rhetorical question, he continued. "I think of myself as a gourmet cook. I'm trying to learn it, anyway. Food is one of the things Clover and I have in common. She likes to eat well, and I like to prepare fancy dishes. Can't you see? We're amazingly compatible that way. You might say we're a natural couple.

"I'll tell you something else. She likes a rub at night and a hot bath after. Got any laws against a man soothing his wife any way she wants? We're married and we're legal age and we're both consenting adults."

"Sprat," Butz interrupted, his voice low, "it looks like you fattened her up for the kill, like a farmer does an animal in a feed lot."

Instead of making Sprat angry, the words seemed to encourage him. "Lieutenant, I'm a smart man. I'd gotten by a long time on my own, before I ever found Clover. Now, put yourself in my place. If you had drifted for years, living on the edge, most always broke, often hungry, sometimes barely keeping ahead of the law, and you found this wonderful woman—like a goose that lays golden eggs—and this female was a pure pleasure to be with; complimenting you and praising you for every little thing, giving you all the money you need, would you hurt her? Would you let anyone else do her harm?" He waited a heartbeat for a response, before providing his own. "Hell, no, you wouldn't. Man, you'd probably feel just like I do. You'd want to watch out for her and protect her and take real good care of that woman. Yes, sir, you would.

"And if that sweet person wanted to go to a concert on a Sunday afternoon, even if you didn't care much for longhair music, you'd load her up and carry her anyway. She'd inspire you. You'd want to do anything for her or with her that she wanted you to do, no questions, no objections."

Butz snorted and there was another long pause. Finally, the lieutenant glanced at Wheeler, then at MaryBeth, inviting their participation.

"What did you see in Clover that you didn't see in Treena, Mr. Sprat?" MaryBeth asked point blank.

He looked at her unabashedly. "Money, Ms. Gilland. That was the first difference I saw between them. Cold, hard cash.

"I did their tax work. Clover lived careful on her trust fund. She'd left it intact. The way it was set up, they couldn't touch the principal anyway, until they married. Clover hadn't ever married, until she married me.

"She had been advised. She knew she probably could have challenged the terms of the trust years ago, but she didn't want to do it. Didn't want to go against their daddy's wishes.

"Treena, on the other hand, went out and hooked herself a man she could put the spurs to long enough to get to that money. That poor slob practically signed his whole life away before they said their 'I do's.' After they'd tied the knot, and it was all official and recognized, she cut him loose. Then she set about living it up, buying everything, most of it useless junk, everything from water beds to water bikes, not that she could use hardly any of that stuff. She bought this big oceangoing boat, then never set a foot on it herself. She's got no business on a boat of any kind. The woman can't even swim.

"Once her pile was gone, most of it anyway, she started making plans for getting her greedy mitts on Clover's money."

At the term "greedy mitts," Wheeler stirred. "You weren't going to stand by and watch that happen, were you? You had plans to for Clover's money, yourself, isn't that right?"

"I'll tell you the truth," Sprat said, the phrase again setting off MaryBeth's warning bells. "I have been living it up. With Clover's money. With Clover. It's like I told you. I don't have to wait around for her to pass and leave it to me. She acts like it's as much mine as hers already. Like I said, she's generous as hell, cash, credit cards, anything. I tell you, she's a giving woman, but at the same time, she's smart about it."

"What does that mean?"

"It means, she knows perfectly well what that sister of hers is after. Clover watched Treena waste her inheritance on all kinds of stupid stuff, including that husband she jettisoned as soon as he'd done what she needed him to do."

Again the room was silent, except for four people breathing.

"Did you know Clover was in the process of changing her will?" Wheeler asked.

Sprat didn't look surprised by the question. "Changing it again, you mean? Yes, sure I knew, but that was none of my business. She changed it once right after we were married."

"Changed it how?"

"I didn't ask. Didn't care, but she told me about it anyway.

"Under the will she told me about, I get half of Clover's money, if she dies before I do. A quarter goes to a nephew. His name's Wayne Tessler. He was Sylvia's boy, the son of Clover and Treena's dead sister. Tessler got left out of their daddy's will. His mom had already passed when their old daddy died. There was no love lost between the old man and Wayne's daddy. The kid never bothered to make any contact with his dead mama's family.

"She and I talked it over. I encouraged her to change it whatever way she wanted to."

"What about the other quarter? Where does it go?"

"She was leaving Treena the other quarter share along with all the family heirlooms, the historical papers and picture albums, the family Bible, old letters and stuff like that. She knew I didn't have any use for their family memorabilia. Clover also knew I would appreciate our apartment and cash money more. She already took care of all that. She looked out for me first."

"So, what's the new change about?" Wheeler tried again.

"Far as I know, it has nothing to do with me. She's brought it up several times, thinking out loud about changes she wanted to make, especially after she and Treena had a blow-up on the telephone one night. When she asked what I thought, I told her I was happy for her to leave me anything she wanted to, but, frankly, I liked things just like they are. I can tell you, psychologically—emotionally—I'm a rocking boat. Clover's my ballast. She's the steady hand that keeps me from tipping over in the stormy seas of life. To be honest, I never have wanted to think too much about Clover passing. She's not that old, you know, and she hasn't had any major health problems, at least, nothing to speak of." He waved off our anticipated objections as all three of the other people in the room inhaled, ready to argue the point.

He shook his head and continued. "I figured we could ditch a few extra pounds, if they got to be a problem. Figured we'd get some warning signs before anything serious happened." He shrugged. "She could always do the will thing later on. I wasn't thinking there was any hurry. I sure didn't encourage her to make any changes my way. I tell you, I'm happy living the life we've got."

MaryBeth, Gray, and Lieutenant Butz sat looking from one of their companions to the other. Wheeler looked like he believed the guy, by the time Sprat began talking again.

"I'll give you an example of how she and I are. We went out for a ride one afternoon, and she told me to pull into this dealership. Without my asking or hinting or even saying a word, she up and bought me that Mercedes. She did choose the color. Said the gray was more distinguished. She paid with a check. Had them put the title in my name. She left her own car right there on the lot so she could ride with me. We haven't been back to get hers yet. She isn't comfortable in my car, but she knows I like that particular make of wheels and what I like is good enough for her.

"That's the way she is. I suspect my being so

happy with her generosity may be what made her want to will me half of her estate in the first place, but I didn't ask her to do it. Like I said, I'm happy the way things are, with the status quo, so to speak."

"So, what happened Sunday night," Butz said, bringing the narrative back to his original train of thought.

Sprat stood and ran his hands down his trousers along his thighs to straighten them, then sat back down.

"Sunday night, I fixed us a big supper about six. Clover likes to eat early on Sunday night. I rinsed the dishes and stuck them in the dishwasher. The maid's off Sundays. Then we played a little gin rummy. Clover's 3,840 points down. We're playing for a dollar a point." He hesitated, grinned at Butz sheepishly, then continued. "Playing for money is her idea, not mine.

"Anyway, we played a little gin and laughed a while, then I took her into her bedroom and we had a little rub, just the way she likes it. Then I ran her a hot bath while she stretched out, recuperating, you might say. After her bath, I patted her down real good with the body powder and lotion she likes. We got her nestled down all cozy and comfy. She asked me if I'd mind going out and getting her a newspaper. She hadn't seen Sunday's paper. Our paper boy forgot us, I guess. Every now and again our Sunday paper is a no-show. It might be one of our neighbors gets off with it, but Clover reads the thing cover to cover, ads and all.

"By the time she thought of it, she was tucked in with the remote control and the *TV Guide* and a bowl of chocolate chip ice cream."

"What time was all this?" Butz asked, jotting in a small notebook he had retrieved from his shirt pocket.

"Probably nine."

"That's when you left?"

"Yeah.

"I couldn't find my keys. I had another set of car keys, but I couldn't find a spare house key, so I left the door unlocked, knowing I'd be right back."

"How long were you gone?" Butz asked.

"A whole lot longer than I planned."

Chapter Seventeen
Sadie

Sprat stood to walk a tight circle, then sat back down. No one else spoke, so he continued his account of what happened that night.

"I ran into an old friend. Sadie Olivia. You people already know about her. She used to live in the rooming house where I lived a while back. She and I are still close. Anyway, Sadie was on her way into the grocery store when I was buying the paper out of a machine outside. I waved her down and we started talking. We got tired of standing there and she offered to fix me a cup of coffee at her place. Going up there took a little longer than I expected. By the time I got home, Clover was sound asleep. I cut off the TV and the lights and smoothed her bed a little. She was sleeping sound. Didn't stir."

"When did you suspect something was wrong?"

"Clover has a sensitive bladder or kidneys or something and she always gets up a couple of times during the night. I sleep listening for her. When she rouses, I usually get up to see about her, turn the lights on and off, like that."

"Do you sleep in the same bed?" MaryBeth interrupted. When all three men looked at her oddly, she shrugged. "I thought it was a pertinent question."

Both Butz and Wheeler nodded, then looked to

Sprat for his answer.

"No, ma'am, we don't." He half smiled. "But my bed's in the same room as hers.

"Anyway, I woke up about five, automatically. Clover's usually been up a couple of times before five. I turned on a lamp and took a look at her. She hadn't moved. I mean, she hadn't budged an inch. Hadn't turned her head or moved a hand. As you probably know, people usually shift some in their sleep. You know what I mean." He glanced at his listeners. They all nodded, as if on cue. "But she hadn't stirred. And she was breathing funny.

"I said her name, but she didn't twitch, so I touched her arm. She still didn't flinch. That scared me. Her pulse was beating in her neck steady as usual. I sat her up and moved her around some, but she didn't respond. Then, I opened her eyelids and checked her pupils.

"I've had a little training, enough to know she was bad off. I didn't even think about calling an ambulance. Later, when I had a chance to think more about it, I decided not calling an ambulance was stupid, especially since I used to drive one. The only thought in my head was getting her to some help.

"I really don't know how I got her to the car. I think I was just so scared, my adrenaline kicked in. All I know is, I drew superhuman strength from some place. I've heard of people doing that in emergencies. Anyway, that's the first time I ever hated my Mercedes.

"I loaded her in the best I could and whipped it over to emergency at Mercy. That's the closest hospital to us. You probably know the rest.

"I'm telling the God's truth about everything that

happened. That's the whole story."

"Were you the one who broke her leg?" Wheeler asked quietly.

Sprat looked at him with wide-eyed sincerity. "I hope to hell not. I was shocked right down to my socks when they told me about that. I don't think I did it, but I can't swear I didn't. Like I said, I was moving out big time. I don't think I slung her into anything, especially not something she would have hit hard enough to break her leg, but I couldn't swear it didn't happen."

Suddenly Sprat's hands were limp and his shoulders slumped again. "Her bones might be brittle, and her age working against her…" He took a breath. "No…honestly, I don't think I did."

Lieutenant Butz frowned at Sprat for a long moment before he cleared his throat.

"Why don't you sit a minute, Mr. Sprat, while Mr. Wheeler and Ms. Gilland and I talk." He motioned Wheeler and MaryBeth to follow as he led them out of the interrogation room and down the hall to a second bleak office. Butz held the door, followed them inside, and closed it.

The room had the same stained wooden floor and was furnished with a square wooden table and four straight-backed wooden chairs. This table, too, was marred with layers of graffiti, carved by idle hands left too long unattended.

"What are we doing in here?" MaryBeth asked.

"Comparing notes," Butz said and indicated she should sit.

She declined, preferring to stay on her feet.

Butz, too, remained standing as Wheeler crumpled into one of the chairs.

"What do you think, Wheeler?" Butz asked, folding his arms across his chest and looking grim.

Wheeler shrugged. "If he wasn't our best suspect, I'd be seriously inclined to believe him. In fact, even the way things are, I believe him." He turned narrowed eyes to MaryBeth. "Do you have any insights?"

"He still has those small hands," she reminded.

Wheeler gave her a caustic grin. "All the better to rub you with, my dear." He flashed a knowing wink at Butz.

MaryBeth frowned. "What does that rub business mean?" Reading their grins, she broke off without finishing the thought. "Never mind."

"Sounds like something you'd like to try sometime? Is that what you're thinking?" Wheeler taunted.

"I said never mind." She scowled. "Has it occurred to either one of you that maybe this isn't even a murder after all?" She turned to Butz. "Are you sure it is, lieutenant?"

Butz regarded her curiously, entertaining the question for several moments. Then he turned to look out the lone window—protected by burglar bars—before drawing a deep breath. "Oh, I think it's murder, all right. One look at that bruise on her leg and the hairs on my neck went on red alert. There are just too many peculiar pieces to this puzzle for it not to be murder. Her broken leg. A paper boy who swears he delivered their Sunday paper at the usual time."

"A neighbor might have picked up the newspaper," MaryBeth offered. "Mine sometimes gets borrowed that way, especially on Sundays."

"Or someone might have taken it intentionally to

get Sprat out of the apartment," Wheeler suggested, showing an interest in the conversation. "Also, it's awfully convenient that Sprat's apartment key disappeared, assuring he'd have to leave the door open if he went anywhere."

Butz frowned, still staring out the window. "So, you're thinking that could all have been planned by some other person or persons? You could be right, looking for someone else to be involved. I'd say we're short on motive with Sprat. Besides, we know he didn't push Ms. Gilland here into that elevator shaft. It looks like he did try to get his wife some immediate medical attention as soon as he realized she needed it."

"Assuming he's telling the truth," MaryBeth said. "I have known a lot of liars who prefaced their biggest lies with phrases like, 'To tell you the truth,' and 'To be perfectly honest.' He used those terms more than once during our interview." She pivoted. "On the other hand, to his credit, he didn't once speak of Clover in the past tense."

"What?" both men said together.

"Sometimes you can tell when grieving people begin to accept the reality of death. The best signal I know is when they begin to refer to the person in the past tense. He doesn't talk about her that way yet. I think if he had planned this and thought he had succeeded in murdering her, he might be doing that."

There was another long silence before MaryBeth had a new thought. "Gray, did he twitch when he told us he couldn't wake her up?"

Gray puckered his mouth and shook his head. "No, but he may be a pro."

"A professional liar? Is there such a thing?"

Gray grimaced. "I can't believe you, a grown woman, don't know that. Especially as good looking as you are. Surely you've heard some big lines."

"Whatever do you mean?"

He glanced at her just as she winked at Butz, and groaned.

"Okay. You got me. But, yes, I still think he's our man." He looked to Butz for confirmation.

Turning his eyes back to the alley outside the one window in the room, Butz nodded. "All we really have is the fact he fattened her up a hundred pounds, give or take." It was the lieutenant's turn to shrug and turn a grimace to his companions. "That's the most incriminating thing against him, and it's a fact he readily admits. One he even seems to take pride in having done."

Gray grunted agreement.

"He was the only one around when she went sour," Butz added. "He could have stood back and let nature take its course instead of racing around getting her to the hospital. I doubt anyone would have blamed him for not realizing she was in such a bad way if she had died."

MaryBeth tapped the nail of one index finger against her front teeth. "At least as far as we know, he was the only person there," she said. "And, of course, we can't discount Gray's ants and the hairs on the back of your neck, Lieutenant."

"I got real strong vibes off that baseball bat," Gray said.

There was a lull in the exchange as each of the trio seemed to be lost in his own puzzling.

"When did you see the baseball bat?" Butz asked

finally, turning a wary eye on Gray. "I cautioned my men specifically not to mention the bat."

Gray ducked his head, apparently trying to come up with an explanation about how he might have seen the bat without admitting his unauthorized visit to the Sprats' apartment. "Forget I said that," he said without looking at either Butz or MaryBeth.

MaryBeth laughed, breaking the ominous tension in the room. "Obviously, Wheeler, you have yet to obtain professional standing as a liar." She chuckled again, wordlessly inviting Butz to share her enjoyment of Gray's discomfort.

Butz gave her a crooked smile, then pulled one of the chairs close to him, sat down and propped his feet on the aged table as his expression again turned grim.

Seeing his mood darken, MaryBeth said, "It's not likely some stranger happened to try the apartment door that evening, precisely during the time Sprat was gone for the paper; that he or she found Clover dozing, found and picked up the baseball bat, cracked her shin—rather than bashing in her noggin—then strolled out without disturbing anything else. Does that make sense to either of you seasoned investigators?"

Both Butz and Gray shook their heads. Slouched in his chair, Gray's shoulders rounded as he crossed his arms over his chest. To MaryBeth, both men looked defeated.

Finally Gray gave her a glum glance. "If someone else had entered the apartment, I doubt Clover would have been alarmed. She would have thought it was Sprat coming back."

"The blow would have roused her," MaryBeth said. "If her attacker wasn't Sprat and Clover thought Sprat was coming right back…"

Butz brightened. "She might not have raised a ruckus or put up a fight…"

"Or tried to call anyone on the phone, which was right there at her bedside…" MaryBeth added.

"It was there later, but maybe it got knocked on the floor or was out of reach during the assault," Gray said.

"She probably figured she could manage until Jack got back," Butz finished.

Gray pursed his lips. "If she has average intelligence, she probably reasoned it out, figured people don't die of a broken leg. She might not have realized her injury could be serious."

"Or that she'd been set up," MaryBeth added. They were silent. "Maybe her assailant was Sadie Olivia," MaryBeth suggested, her voice almost reverent.

"No good," Gray said. "Sadie was with Sprat. Remember?"

Still on her feet, MaryBeth leaned against the wall and folded her arms at her waist. She was having odd vibes each time Sadie's name was mentioned.

Butz took a breath. "They alibi each other. Maybe they did it together. Maybe she was the one who shoved you into the elevator shaft."

"I don't think so. Her hands are more long and slender," MaryBeth said.

"When did you see Sadie?" Gray's tone sounded like an accusation.

"With you, of course. At Bonicellis Theater and Supper Club. Remember?"

He nodded and winced at the same time. "I remembered her. I forgot you were with me, all dressed down like some bag lady."

163

As if trying to short circuit an argument, Lieutenant Butz said, "Maybe our suspect is someone we don't know about yet."

Both Gray and MaryBeth turned their glowering looks on him. It was MaryBeth who rallied first. "Do you mean like maybe it's a neighbor or a maintenance person working at the apartments?"

"No motive." Butz shook his head and growled. He stood up, paced to a corner of the room and curled his shoulders as he leaned his back against the wall, folding his arms over his chest, mirroring MaryBeth.

Gray shifted his chair to allow him to see his companions, then frowned from one to the other. "If Sprat's not our man, whoever used the bat may be concerned about Clover's regaining consciousness, figuring she'll be able to identify him."

"Or her," MaryBeth said.

"Uh-oh." Gray shot a look at MaryBeth and suddenly he jumped up and scurried toward the door. "My ants are moving. Let's get over to the hospital."

Both MaryBeth and Lieutenant Butz followed Gray from the room and right past the waiting Leland Jack Sprat. The civilian detectives stepped into the elevator. Butz lagged behind.

"What about Sprat?" Butz asked in a stage whisper before the elevator doors began to close, separating him from them.

"We'd probably better take him with us," Gray said and stuck one hand between the elevator doors to prevent their closing.

"I'll get him," Butz said, indicating Gray and MaryBeth should hold the elevator. "Wait right here."

Chapter Eighteen
Truth

Butz pulled the police cruiser into the emergency room driveway and stopped. All four occupants clamored out as a nurse came through the automatic doors pushing a wheelchair.

"Are you ambulatory?" she asked crisply.

"Yes, and on a mission," Wheeler said as they swept by her.

"You people are not supposed to come through this entrance unless you need emergency assistance," she called after them. "You cannot park here. This is for patients who need…" She got no response as the four new arrivals disappeared around the corner beyond the admissions desk.

"Should someone wait down here to keep watch?" MaryBeth asked.

Wheeler stopped mid step and whirled to look at her. "Why?"

"To make sure no one slips by us."

"Who?"

She shrugged.

"Keep up," he snapped.

She trotted to catch up and slid into the elevator just as Lieutenant Butz pushed "8" on the selection board.

As they stepped off the elevator on the eighth floor,

they were surprised to find the nurse's station deserted. Sprat took off, trotting through the waiting room and down the hall to Room 817. He stopped just short of colliding with Dr. Tate.

"What's happened?" Sprat asked.

Dr. Tate shook his head. "I'm sorry, Mr. Sprat. Your wife has expired."

"She's dead?" MaryBeth echoed, trying to keep the shock out of her voice. "Oh, no."

Dr. Tate nodded and looked at each of the others. Stumbling back several steps, as if he'd taken a punch, Leland Jack Sprat slumped against the wall and buried his face in his hands. A moment later, he began making little choking noises as he slid down the wall to a squat.

Trying not to look at him, MaryBeth bit her lip and bowed her head. She didn't want to add to the man's anguish.

"Doctor," Wheeler asked, his voice low, "does Treena Flowers know yet?"

"Yes," Dr. Tate said quietly. "She just left."

Wheeler grabbed MaryBeth's wrist and, yanking her rudely, darted back toward the bank of elevators. "Come with me."

Startled out of her doldrums by his odd behavior, she jogged through the hall beside him, barely dodging a food service cart.

They rode the elevator down in silence. As the doors opened on the main floor, they spotted the familiar figure at the same time.

"There she is," MaryBeth said under her breath.

Treena Flowers trudged along, moving away from them, several yards down the hallway. When she realized they were behind her, she stopped and turned around. Drawing a shuddering breath, she squared herself to face them. With no warning, she staggered backward. It appeared she might fall. Instead, she sank almost gracefully onto a bench nearby. She snatched a tissue from her purse and began blowing her nose and dabbing at her eyes. Her breathing came in irregular gasps as if she were sobbing, and her face was more flushed than previous meetings.

As they approached, their client's mouth twisted, distorted in what appeared to be an effort to smile. Their steps in sync, Gray and MaryBeth paced forward, each evaluating, trying to read Treena Flowers' reaction.

"I am very sorry for your loss," Wheeler began.

Mrs. Flowers nodded and seemed to be gathering herself to respond. As she continued wiping her eyes with the tissue, she dug a fist into the purse she juggled on her lap, produced a checkbook and, after drawing several deep, quivering breaths, opened it and began to write.

When she finished, she thrust a check toward Gray, who took it and stared down at it. The check was payable to Your Eyes Only Detectives in the amount of seven thousand dollars.

Mrs. Flowers said, "That's five thousand for the arrest of that awful man, and one thousand dollars a day for the two partial days you have been in my employ."

MaryBeth stared into the woman's face. There was no moisture. Neither current tears, nor traces of recent weeping were visible. Her face was flushed where she had scrubbed it with the tissue. Strangely enough, Treena's nose didn't need attention either, nor was there moisture in the corners of her mouth.

"When he's convicted of murdering my precious sister," the woman said quietly, "I will pay you the additional ten thousand, as promised."

Suddenly Treena Flowers exploded with what sounded like hoarse, gulping sobs, covering her face with the tissue clutched tightly in one paunchy hand. Her bosom shook and her shoulders trembled. Her face was hidden.

"Clover," Mrs. Flowers called out, her voice muffled, "my own sweet, dear sister. Come back to me, dearest." Blinking, she turned her face toward Wheeler. "I'm left here alone. Clover, the only other survivor of our original family, is gone. I am abandoned to face the world alone. Mother and Daddy, baby Sylvia, and now, precious, precious Clover, all taken from me. What does it mean that I am the only one remaining? Is there something God has prepared for me to do?" She peered over her fist and up, as if looking for an answer from Gray, who stood over her frowning. MaryBeth noticed that the woman's eyes remained remarkably dry.

MaryBeth stepped around Gray, lowered herself onto the bench beside Treena, and fished around in her own purse for a clean tissue. When she found one, she shook it out and offered it to their client.

Without attempting to speak, Treena nodded appreciation and reached for the offered tissue.

Straightening, MaryBeth abruptly withdrew the offer. She looked up at Gray, realization washing through her. She made no attempt to hide what she was thinking.

He bent close to MaryBeth as Mrs. Flowers waved a limp hand, blindly groping for the tissue that was offered, then withdrawn. "What is it?" he whispered near MaryBeth's ear, obviously puzzled by her gesture.

MaryBeth pointed both her index fingers at Flowers' small, pudgy hand.

His eyes rounded as he caught her meaning. "Oh, yeah. I see."

Mrs. Flowers didn't notice the exchange.

"Do you think you will be able to satisfy a jury that Jack killed Clover?" she sputtered. She didn't appear to register MaryBeth's withdrawal of the tissue.

When neither Gray nor MaryBeth answered, Flowers looked up, blinking as if unable to see clearly or, maybe, encouraging tears. "What I mean is, can you prove the bastard murdered my sister and deprived me of my only living relative?"

MaryBeth sat staring at their client, unmoving, puzzling, feeling as if her psyche had been slapped. How could she not have suspected Treena? Every coincidence, every morsel of evidence pointed at her, the sister who would inherit one-fourth of Clover's estate? Unless, of course, she could find a way to disinherit the husband and take his half as well, disregarding entirely her nephew Wayne Tessler. Was money what this was all about?

MaryBeth needed time to figure this out. Could Treena have accomplished all this alone? Without an accessory?

Gray cleared his throat, pulling her out of her deliberations, as he addressed Treena's question. "A prosecutor will have no trouble proving Jack made her fat. Sprat not only admits it, he even brags about doing it. Prosecutors also can show that Clover's obesity contributed to her death."

As Wheeler spoke, his words coming slowly,

MaryBeth eased closer to Ms. Flowers and inhaled, trying to establish another element identifying the culprit who had pushed her into the elevator shaft.

As if totally absorbed in his words, Flowers gazed up at Gray, fluttering her eyelashes. "Does that mean he'll be held responsible for her death?" She seemed, suddenly, to be in total command of her emotions. "Does that mean the bastard will be convicted of murder?"

Gray Wheeler looked at MaryBeth as he answered. "No, Mrs. Flowers, I'm afraid there is no law against making someone fat. If there were, half the population in this country would be crime victims."

Mrs. Flowers struggled to stand. Once she was up, she assumed a militant posture, feet wide, knees locked as if positioning herself to do battle. "What about the baseball bat? What about that? And Clover's broken leg?" Her face contorted into a scathing expression of accusation and hate. All signs of overwhelming grief—present only the moment before—had vanished. MaryBeth studied the older woman, mouth agape. Meanwhile, Gray's expression changed from troubled to enlightened as his eyes tracked from Treena to MaryBeth, then back to the older woman.

At that moment, MaryBeth and Gray shared an epiphany—a moment of sudden insight—requiring no verbal exchange. A single conclusion.

Gray's voice was soft as he said, "What baseball bat would that be, Mrs. Flowers?"

Treena looked startled for a moment, glancing up and down the corridor. There were no other people. She appeared to be reassessing her statement and reaching a decision, whereupon, she again plopped down on the bench and buried her face in the wad of tissue. She scrubbed her eyes and resumed her wailing, obviously stalling.

Gray gave MaryBeth a knowing look and a nod.

The older woman babbled into her hands, then stammered as she raised her head and began to speak to them, audibly, again.

"Why…why, the baseball bat you mentioned finding at Clover's." She gave Gray a watery smile, but the effort was lost on him. Blinking prettily, an effort that might have been effective on a woman half her age and size, Flowers then flashed a pleading glance at MaryBeth, who pretended not to notice the appeal.

Gray's voice had a brittle resonance as he spoke. "Mrs. Flowers, I have not said anything to you about a baseball bat."

"Well, then, ah, I suppose it was Ms. Gilland. Yes, I think I remember now, it was MaryBeth who mentioned it." She again glanced toward MaryBeth, a plea for assistance.

Experiencing another epiphany, MaryBeth inhaled again, analyzing the familiar fragrance as her mind took off on another rabbit trail. Surprising Gray and Treena both, MaryBeth suddenly grabbed Mrs. Flowers' wrists.

"These are the hands!" MaryBeth announced triumphantly, jutting her jaw, daring Gray to argue as she set a fixed stare on him.

Treena Flowers jerked her hands out of MaryBeth's grip. "Have you lost your mind?"

Wheeler looked from one woman to the other before his eyes settled on MaryBeth. "The ones in your dreams?" he asked, apparently confused.

"No. The ones that shoved me into the elevator

shaft in the hallway outside the newspaper library. Do you remember my telling you about the sickening sweet aftershave?"

"Yes."

"It was sickening when I thought it was a man's after shave, but it's rather pleasant as a woman's cologne."

Wheeler looked at the heavy woman, gauging her with renewed interest. "Mrs. Flowers shoved you into the elevator shaft?"

"Less than twenty-four hours after she apparently slugged her own poor sister with a baseball bat," MaryBeth said, glowering first at her partner, before she turned that dark look on their new suspect.

Treena stared. "Don't be ridiculous. I have no idea what you're referring to. I can also assure you, these hands have never so much as touched a baseball bat. I loved Clover. If you recall, it was I who hired you, for heaven's sake, to investigate this atrocity. Who would hire private detectives to investigate a crime she herself was in the middle of committing? This crime—this tragic homicide—would have gone unnoticed if I had not called it to everyone's attention."

Flowers again struggled to her feet, her ending stance again militant.

"If I had wanted to murder my own sister, would I have hounded the police trying to get them focused on what was going on in the Sprats' home? Would I have fought so hard to have that wicked man banished from her house and out of her life?"

Wheeler turned a quizzical look on MaryBeth. "Yeah, what about that?"

MaryBeth bit her lip, sizing up the man, trying to

calm herself. "Wheeler, did I question your ants? Did I dispute your twitches or the hair bristling on Lieutenant Butz's neck? Do not argue with me about hands or fragrances.

"Besides, she didn't call us in to investigate anything until the deed was all but done, while she was twiddling her thumbs, waiting for the death knell."

Angrily, Ms. Flowers spun to face Wheeler. "You're a logical man, Mr. Wheeler. Am I the kind of woman who could have orchestrated a plan that depended on Clover falling for some gigolo, at her age? How in the world would I have arranged for them to meet without alerting everyone at Younger and Zale? How could I have perpetuated events that would culminate in their marriage? For God's sake, man, be rational. Could anyone other than the two principals involved have anticipated, much less arranged that scenario? Absolutely not!"

She hoisted her satchel and purse from the bench.

"It wasn't I who fed her until she was so fat she could scarcely move. I wasn't the one rolling her around in a wheelchair to limit her walking, or pampering her until she resembled some gigantic religious idol, so fat that a single blow to her shin could cause her death.

"I would never—could never—have planned something as ludicrous as that. I have no knowledge of human physiology."

MaryBeth watched Ms. Flowers as the woman spoke, listening with all her senses. Then realization slithered through her mind.

"She used him!" MaryBeth's voice reflected her own amazement and, at the same time a hint of regard.

Gesturing toward Treena, MaryBeth's voice rose. "She duped Sprat from the beginning. Tricked him into being a red herring, diverting everyone's attention. Not just ours, but law enforcement's. And Clover's too." She focused a puzzled look on Wheeler, an appeal for him to chime in and clarify her thinking. "Why did Treena hire us?"

He gave her a knowing smile. "I believe we may be just now shining some light on this whole caper. I suspect Treena has a coconspirator, all right, but I don't believe it's Jack.

"Treena and her accomplice may have planned Clover's demise together, but not from the beginning. I imagine Treena's original plan, to be accomplished alone, was for Sprat to romance Clover and encourage her to loosen her grip on her inheritance. But things got complicated, and Treena saw she needed another player on her side. So, she recruited one."

"Who?"

Wheeler gave her a crooked smile. "You and I were practically convinced Sprat was the villain, and we kept trying to direct the evidence toward him. At least we did until we learned that Clover planned to change her will…again."

Treena Flowers stiffened and again made direct eye contact with Wheeler. "I am a primary beneficiary under any will Clover has ever had," she said, joining their conversation. "I always have been. The bulk of her estate is mine."

"That's not so," Wheeler said.

MaryBeth eased a step back from the determined-looking Treena. "Apparently, Clover drew up a new will after she and Jack married. The way we understand it, under the revision, you and Wayne each inherit family heirlooms along with one-fourth of the cash in her estate. Jack is to receive the apartment and its contents, half of the cash, and any vehicles."

"No!" Treena shouted. "There's never been a will like that."

"Oh, yes, I believe there is," Wheeler said. "It will be the one presented for probate."

"When did that happen?" Treena's voice had become a screech.

"Clover made a new will a month after she and Jack married." Wheeler seemed to relish providing that information and watching Treena squirm and wilt. Finally, she shook her head so hard, her hair shifted. She appeared to be wearing a wig. She righted the arrangement on her head but was not distracted from their conversation or its startling revelations.

"Apparently, your nagging and finding fault with Jack finally riled your even-tempered sister. Indications are she was changing her will to leave Jack everything. Cutting you and your nephew out entirely."

MaryBeth flashed Wheeler a look as she interrupted. "So, are you saying Wayne Tessler is his Aunt Treena's coconspirator?"

Wheeler grinned. "Good guess, partner, but wrong. Think about the set up."

She frowned.

"Do you want a hint?"

"Yes," she said.

"Hell hath no fury like…?"

"A woman scorned. But we've already figured out Treena had the most to gain." She brightened. "Ahhh. Jack's occasional girlfriend, a woman who didn't like always playing second fiddle. You're suggesting Sadie and Treena were in cahoots. Will Sadie tell?"

"Now you're on the right track. Also, I'm pretty sure Sadie can be persuaded to talk."

MaryBeth turned as she and Wheeler both looked at Treena.

If looks could kill, MaryBeth Gilland might have expired at that moment in the face of Treena Flowers' murderous glare.

"What I don't understand," MaryBeth said, frowning, "is why this woman pushed me into an elevator shaft."

"She got a little heavy-handed with that." He hesitated, allowing time for MaryBeth to appreciate his pun.

She grimaced.

"The truth is, Treena turned our whole investigation around with that one bonehead move." He looked at Treena. "We had Sprat pretty well nailed as the culprit until then. But Butz holding him at the police station for questioning that afternoon gave him a perfect alibi."

Wheeler turned his attention back to MaryBeth. "I believe Treena gave you the shove to implicate Sprat in an effort to keep him from divulging the rough-draft plan she had outlined for him before she set her plan in motion. She had no idea, of course, that Sprat would have such an ironclad alibi. She should have paid better attention to details."

"Can we prove any of this? Do we have any provable case against Treena at all?"

They both swung around to look at Treena Flowers. She lowered her eyes to stare at the wadded tissue in her hands, as if she had lost interest in their conversation. They could neither see her face nor read her thoughts by her expression.

"I don't think so," Gray said, under his breath. "The only witness we have to the elevator shaft incident is you. Your description of the man's small hands and his sweet smelling aftershave are in the official police report. No one's going to recognize that as a description of Treena Flowers."

Treena appeared to have shifted to listening mode again. She looked from Wheeler to MaryBeth, her expression changing from indifferent to triumphant.

"Besides that, I am your client," she said. "It was I who invited you into this matter in the first place. You were hired to look out for my interests. My communications with you are privileged. Any information you obtained from my private disclosures—like my little slip about the baseball bat—certainly is covered by our employer/employee relationship."

She smiled.

A stir at the end of the hall drew their attention as Pepper Butz and Leland Jack Sprat burst through the outside doors and strode down the hall toward them in lock step.

"Treena Flowers," Butz called from the end of the corridor, "you are under arrest for the murder of Clover Sprat."

Chapter Nineteen
Suspects

MaryBeth Gilland looked first at Lieutenant Butz, then glanced at Leland Jack Sprat. She also snapped a quick peek at Treena Flowers before her puzzled eyes settled, finally, on Gray Wheeler.

Butz strode straight into Treena's space and pulled up short. He did not touch her as he read her rights in a clear, baritone voice. "I have a full confession from your cohort here," Butz said. "He's explained the whole conspiracy...your plan."

"Seriously?" Treena said, "Are the rantings and suppositions of a bereaved husband all you've got?"

"While he may have listened to your original idea, Mrs. Flowers, nothing he did appears to have been illegal or immoral, much less criminal."

"Lieutenant," Flowers all but drawled, "I'm sure you've noticed—" She hesitated as the outside doors opened and two uniformed officers stepped in. MaryBeth and Gray glanced at the new arrivals before turning back to their client.

"I met Treena first," Sprat interjected. "Before I ever even saw Clover. It was in the summer of 2007. I'd just lost my wife, Margaret." Sprat glared at Treena. "I should have known right off the kind of woman Treena was.

"We met in an X-rated movie on a Friday

afternoon. Treena knew who I was, and that I had been married to Margaret Swenson. It wasn't until later that Treena told me she followed me into the theater that afternoon. There were only a handful of people in the whole place. She came directly to the row where I was sitting and sat right down in the empty seat next to me. She wasn't there for the feature.

"We'd been there a few minutes when Treena put her hand on my thigh. I just sat there like a bump on a log."

"That's not all that happened!" Treena erupted, again on her feet and looking combative.

"Here, now," Lieutenant Butz said, stepping between Flowers and Sprat. "We'll hear from you in just a minute."

Sprat gave Flowers a smug I-told-you-so look. "In the theater, she leaned close and began whispering very specific, very naughty, suggestive things in my ear.

"Between her racy talk and the heavy breathing and nudity on the screen, I got to feeling cooperative. She invited me to accompany her to a place nearby. She said it belonged to a friend who was out of town.

"Under the lights in the lobby, I got a better look at her, and my interest waned. I mean, she wasn't exactly...my...type. I was about to turn her down, but then she offered me five hundred dollars for an hour of my time and a little conversation.

"I was not only hard at the time, I was also hard up, for cash. I didn't see any harm in going along with her. I mean it was a slow day with not much going on, and my morale was in the dumper.

"Treena was all over me the minute we closed the door to that apartment."

Flowers huffed loudly. Butz frowned at her, and she neither stood up nor spoke.

"I didn't manhandle her or anything, but I had to forcefully push her to arm's length. I told her she had the wrong idea about me…us.

"She said she found me attractive and, from gossip she had heard about my marriage, she assumed I was good in the sack."

"That's a damned lie," Flowers had sat, but she shouted and struggled to her feet again. "I never said I thought he'd be any good in bed. Barely adequate would be more like it."

Treena's eyes locked with Sprat's for a moment before he grinned.

"She also assumed I had a weakness for rich older babes." He paused a moment, still grinning at her. "That's how she referred to herself. As a babe."

Treena began to tremble and her face turned bright red.

"She pulled five one-hundred-dollar-bills out of her pocket and peeled them off in my hand. She said there was plenty more where that came from. She said if I was interested, she might have a job for me, one that paid well and fit my particular skills.

"I didn't see any harm in listening. I mean five crisp Ben Franklins can get a guy's attention."

Sprat's knowing grin had her fisting her hands and flailing her arms, threatening him there in the hospital corridor. One of the patrolmen nearby responded to the lieutenant's signal, caught both of Treena's wrists and cuffed them behind her. That's when MaryBeth noticed their group had drawn the attention of several people in the hospital lobby.

"Maybe we should take this interview someplace a little more private," she said, indicating the audience.

"Just leaving. Officers, transport these two to the office, in separate vehicles, understand?" The patrolmen nodded.

"Get my purse," Treena ordered. One of the policemen moved to follow her order as the other escorted Jack to the patrol cars.

"Do you want to go?" Gray asked, speaking to MaryBeth.

"Yes. If it's all right with the lieutenant."

Both looked at the officer.

"I don't know if we've got a case here, or not," Butz said with a shrug. "It will probably take all three of us to put this thing together. I appreciate your offering. Come along."

****

Sprat and Flowers were kept separate until they were all seated in one interview room, the suspects at opposite ends of a long wooden table.

No one spoke as Wheeler, Gilland, and Butz settled at the sides of the table. Butz broke the silence.

"What happened next in the apartment?"

"Treena described this plan of hers where I would romance her sister Clover, help talk her into sharing her wealth with Treena, who was low on funds. If her plan worked, Treena would pay me ten grand. The deal sounded okay. First step in Treena's plan was for me to interview with Younger and Zale. It was tax season and they were happy to get a referral from a client, especially since I could show them some credentials.

"I worked hard, happy for the opportunity. I also snooped through old tax records there in the office. I found out right off that Treena and Clover had both inherited big time from their deceased daddy. Two million apiece. A quarter of a million of that was transferred to each in cash. The rest of it was in investments through an old-line brokerage house. Their dad had put the investments in a trust. His daughters had to marry before they could tap into the big money.

"Treena got married with a prenup, then kicked the guy loose as soon as she got the money out of the trust. By the time I met her, Treena's share—cash and investments—was all but gone, which is why she was looking to share in her sister's pot of gold. Clover's inheritance had scarcely been touched. Mostly, Clover lived off the dividends and interest. Even her cash was making money. She was a careful spender. Not a Scrooge, you understand, but thrifty.

"When I saw what she had, I got to thinking about the deal Treena had offered. What did I need Treena for? When I asked her that, she tried to get all kissy-face again. I wasn't interested in that action with her, not even with big bucks for an incentive.

"Before the end of that week, she showed up in my office at Younger and Zale with her sister. I got the impression Clover was 'bait.'"

"That's my sister you're talking about!" Treena chose that moment to shove her chair back from the table in the closed interrogation room. Lieutenant Butz's eyes narrowed as he looked at her. He raised one hand to the table and tapped the handcuffs he'd removed upon arrival.

Sprat kept talking. "Treena obviously was looking for me to get in line, but things did not go according to her plan."

Treena slumped back into her chair.

Sprat looked at Treena. When her gaze met his, he arched his eyebrows. "First thing, I genuinely liked Clover. Not only was she pretty, she was shy and quiet and…well, she just had a real sweet disposition, if you know what I mean." After general round of nods in the room, minus Treena's, he continued. "Clover was sincere and straightforward. I mean she was nothing like her sister. Totally unaffected. It didn't hurt, of course, that I had verified the woman was seriously rich. To tell you the truth, I got interested right off. I mean the woman had most of the qualities I consider attractive in a person of the opposite sex. I asked her out. She was tactful, but it was obvious guys had made moves on her money before. She asked me if this was a social engagement or a business dinner. I told her it was purely social.

"We had a real good time together that night. Went out for steaks. She asked me about myself and she listened to what I said. She asked legitimate questions and she paid attention to the answers, like she was interested in my stories and maybe me personally. So, what the heck, I decided, and I told her some deeper personal stuff, even threw in a few of the occurrences in my life I'm not proud about. She shed the bad stuff like water off a duck's back. I mean, she's not someone who condemns a person for minor crimes and misdemeanors in their past. We stayed up almost all night talking like that. Open.

"When Clover and I had gone out two or three times, Treena called me up to talk more about her scheme." He hesitated, staring at nothing in particular.

MaryBeth studied him, the timbre in his voice, his

facial expressions, his body language. "She was talking to you about a plot to murder her sister, and you were going along with it, as happy as a clam?"

Sprat's eyes rounded as they met hers in obvious disapproval.

"No, no, no, ma'am. There was never any talk about killing anyone. And I did not go along with anything, at least not on her terms."

"You wanted to negotiate the split? Understandable. How much did you demand, Mr. Sprat?"

"I suggested Treena pay me a percentage of whatever she was able to glom onto. It could be a little or a lot. The way she talked and from what I'd figured out already, Clover was still going to have plenty."

"Did Treena agree to give you a percentage of the eventual haul?" Detective Butz asked.

"No, she did not. She was even rude about it. I thought that was pretty stupid of her. After all, the way things were going, she was just so much extra baggage in the deal. I could probably cut her out altogether."

"He overestimated himself...as usual." Treena drew a breath as if she were winding up to say more, but Butz shook an index finger at her.

"You'll have your turn, Ms. Flowers. You be quiet now, or we'll have you escorted out of the room."

Treena bit her lip and nodded, but the look she gave Sprat dripped with venom.

"You were willing to pretend to go along with her plan?" Butz continued the questioning. He sounded skeptical. "Killing a woman you professed to love, or at least admire, on the come?"

Sprat's eyebrows veed and his voice rose, startling

everyone in the room. "THERE WAS NO TALK OF KILLING ANYONE. In all our discussions, no one ever suggested that. I did tell Treena I'd need ten thousand dollars front money, to give me pocket cash for necessities. I wouldn't have agreed to kill a living person for any amount, for sure not for a measly ten grand."

"Did Mrs. Flowers agree to do things your way?"

"No. She wouldn't even agree to give me any cash money up front," Sprat said. "Truth was, she didn't have it. She offered me jewelry instead. Her good jewelry was already gone. She slipped two pieces out of Clover's jewelry box. It was quality stuff. I took it to a pawn shop guy who knows. He valued those two at a total of around five grand. If you know anything about pawn brokers, you know they estimate low."

"Did you sell or pawn the pieces?" Butz asked.

"Neither one. No, sir. I held onto them thinking I could get something for my trouble out of them later on, if Treena's plan blew up in her face. Or, I was thinking I might want to return them to Clover later, depending on how things lined up."

"So you agreed to conspire to take your wife's property, maybe even her life?" MaryBeth breathed quietly.

His eyes darted to MaryBeth's face. "How many times have I got to tell you? No one said anything about her dying. I don't know why you keep throwing that out there. Clover's dying was never part of it. Can't you understand? I was crazy about the woman."

"So, what were some of Treena's ideas?"

"All I had to do was indulge Clover—make the woman happy. One of Treena's ideas was to get Clover boozing until she was incapacitated; not able to make sound decisions on her own. The idea was to get her to a point that maybe she'd need a guardian of her person and her property. The natural one for a judge to appoint would be her sister, her next of kin."

"Not her husband?"

"Marriage was not part of any of Treena's original notions. I was supposed to court Clover, maybe move in with her, if she wanted me to, but neither Treena nor I thought about my marrying her sister. That sort of came about on its own." Sprat stretched his arms and legs, rotated his wrists, and bent his fingers.

"To be honest with you, the last thing I ever expected was to fall in love." He stopped talking and looked down to frown at the floor, as if he were still puzzling over that turn of events. He sucked in air, sort of gasping, and looked as if he were struggling about something. The next thing that happened was tears. They seeped out of the corners of his eyes. MaryBeth looked away, afraid his tears again might prompt tears of her own.

Butz cleared his throat. "You didn't expect Clover to fall in love with you?"

"Sure I did." Sprat raised his eyes to the lieutenant's face. "That was the idea. We expected her to fall for me. The surprise was me falling for her."

Butz and Wheeler nodded in unison as MaryBeth said a breathy, "I see."

Sprat still didn't make eye contact with any of the other people in the room. He just began talking again. "It was easy to see how we might be compatible, what with me being a gourmet cook and Clover liking to eat."

Shifting in her chair, Treena groaned with disbelief.

"Also, I was an accountant. I liked fooling with money—investing and handling people's funds. Clover had plenty to make my studying markets and selecting funds worthwhile. My being sort of what I considered a bad boy and her having a forgiving nature also worked for us. You can see, we were a natural match.

"My plan was to woo her, spoil her a little, and maybe move in with her, then get her to loosen up with her money. I came up with several ideas for reducing her income taxes. One was by gifting money to her sister and this Wayne Tessler. He was her nephew, the son of their dead sister. The guy lives right here in town now. That way, those two of her kin could have extra walking around money every year, and Clover would get the tax benefit from being generous.

"What I didn't think about was that to Treena, ten thousand dollars was chump change."

He paused again. No one else in the room spoke, so after a little delay, Sprat continued.

"Like I said, Clover was easy to like. It didn't take long for me to get sincerely fond of her. And she was happy with me. The crazy thing was, no matter what I told her about my past, she praised me. She thought I was energetic and smart and resourceful. She credited me with all kinds of attributes she saw in me, things I never even considered were good traits. The more she bragged on me, the better I was. I loved the me she saw...the me I was turning out to be. You can see how our friendship...relationship...you know...developed. I needed her. She needed me. We related so well, our relationship was sort of a natural progression. Pretty soon, I asked her to marry me."

"Spontaneously?" MaryBeth asked.

"Right out of the blue," Sprat continued, ignoring the interruption. "One afternoon while we were watching the news on TV. Surprised us both. She said yes. I turned off the TV right then. The only trouble with the whole beautiful arrangement was Treena. The woman pitched a walleyed fit.

"On the sly I told her Clover and me being married would make Treena's plan for getting her hands on Clover's money work even better because I would be right there at her side encouraging Clover to share. Her being married meant she would be able to get into the bulk of her money in the trust."

"I've never heard a bigger pile of crap in my life," Treena shouted. "Why would I need some bum off the street to con my sister out of her money? I was her only heir already. I was going to inherit her entire fortune. I didn't need anyone else's help."

"But," Butz said, "you only inherited if Clover died. She was trundling right along, hale and hearty, and about to be married. Husbands usually inherit in front of sisters. Besides, I'm thinking the green-eyed monster had a hold on you. I'm thinking you not only wanted your sister's money. You wanted her man. Isn't that a fact?"

The woman sat quivering for a moment before she sneered. "I may have been the tiniest bit jealous at one time." She paused. "Now that I think about it, you may be right. It wasn't just Clover's money I wanted, but it wasn't him. I did envy the way he paid so much attention to her, but I pushed that out of my head when he told me he had fallen in love with her. With Clover?

A man like Jack in love with a blimp like her? He might have her fooled, but he couldn't con me. I didn't know who he thought he was fooling. I saw right straight through him. All he saw in her was dollar signs."

Sprat sputtered, attempting to object, but Treena waved him down. "It didn't take long to confirm what he was up to when Clover mentioned she was in the process of changing her Will. Obviously Sprat planned to replace my plan with one of his own. He didn't bother to tell you that, did he? He planned to leave me out of our arrangement altogether."

"You expected me to *kill her*!" Sprat shouted. "I told you that wasn't going to happen. Not only was I not going to murder Clover, I wasn't going to let anyone else hurt her, either." He addressed others in the room. "I promised Treena that right then. I flat wasn't going to let it happen."

"What he actually said was, there was no hurry," Treena Flowers corrected calmly. "He said there was no need to harm her physically, when all we needed to do was wait and let nature take its course."

"I never said anything of the kind," Sprat shouted as he took a step toward her, his anger flaring all over again.

Her voice was low, her eyes narrowing as she addressed the lieutenant. "That's what I heard, Lieutenant Butz."

"Did you hear those words from him, or did you get that information second hand?" Butz asked.

"Let's say it came from a very reliable source."

Butz studied Treena a moment, but the pause seemed brief. "Then you admit you planned to have your sister assassinated. Is that what you're telling the

189

people in this room right now?"

Treena Flowers looked from Butz to Wheeler to MaryBeth, then pursed her lips. "I invested everything I had—my last dollar—in setting him up. I bought him clothes and accessories he insisted he needed for courting her. I had to get my investment back. He told me to keep track of my expenditures in his behalf. Said he'd repay me off the top of whatever we got. We'd split the rest, fifty-fifty. Can you imagine the gall? He expected me to give him half of an inheritance that should rightfully come to me. It was absurd. He was a salaried employee. As we haggled, I believe he began to realize that. I needed the larger share. I had a lifestyle to maintain."

She leveled a hard look at Sprat. "Jack Sprat was and is a prostitute, a high-dollar lover for hire, but you had to be able to afford him.

She returned her attention to the others, as Sprat's face flamed.

"One night as I sat parked across the street watching their apartment, he came out of the building and got in his car. I followed him. That's when I discovered what an animal he was. That's when I found out he had no honor. No integrity. No loyalty. Not to me, not to Clover, not to anyone.

"He met that tramp. That Sadie." She rolled her eyes. "Oh, they were a match, all right. She was a whore calling herself a model, and he was a gigolo calling himself a tax consultant."

"A woman scorned," MaryBeth said quietly.

"Is that when you planned Clover's demise?" Butz asked. "When you came up with the idea of setting him up? You were the one who got him out of the apartment last Sunday night and set up the circumstances that left the apartment door unlocked. Is that how you were able to sneak in and slug Clover with the baseball bat?"

MaryBeth felt a chill as Treena turned a murderous gaze on her.

"The only thing I'm guilty of is hitting my sister," Treena Flowers said. "It was simple assault, at the worst. What siblings haven't had similar experiences?"

"Inside," Treena continued, "the handsome Leland Jack Sprat is no more than a common thug. He has no pedigree, no honor. I did not want my sister to die. No one would wish their last blood relative in the world dead. I may have wanted her temporarily incapacitated, but that was the extent of my ill will. Clover was my own flesh and blood."

Lieutenant Butz stared at the floor.

"I had no motive for killing her," Flowers insisted.

"You did if you are her heir," Sprat reminded her.

When Treena leapt to her feet, the two policemen standing just inside the door went on alert. Butz caught Treena's hand and snapped the cuffs on her.

"I told you Clover was too good for me," Sprat shouted, to no one in particular. "I never deserved anyone as sweet as her. The woman was my life! I loved her!"

Treena spat toward him but was twisted the wrong way to make the gesture more than an insult.

Butz motioned the two officers to remove Treena Flowers from the room. Wheeler looked at Butz.

"What about Sprat?" he asked, indicating the man crumpled at the table sobbing quietly.

"On Flowers," Butz said, "we have an assault that resulted in a death. That's felony murder. The case would be stronger if she had taken the weapon to the apartment with her, but we'll try to convince the district attorney to go with what we've got. We might be able to charge Sprat as an accomplice, but except for Ms. Flowers' ravings, the only actual evidence we've got on him is overindulging his wife. Far as I can find, that's no crime."

"Nothing else?" MaryBeth asked, suddenly indignant.

"He was living in the lap of luxury. I imagine he liked the status quo. I can't see that he had any motive to do her harm. Nothing to gain." He turned to Sprat. "You're free to go now, Mr. Sprat."

Sprat lifted his head and blinked at the others, as if he'd been somewhere else entirely. Slowly he stood, mumbled his thanks, and avoided eye contact with them all. As he turned to leave and his shoulders rounded, a slight smile lifted Sprat's mouth, although he kept his eyes set firmly on the floor. With no restraints, he shuffled through the interrogation room door, down the hall, and disappeared into an elevator. As the door behind him closed, MaryBeth was reminded of her own near miss that morning.

"Was Sadie involved in any of this?" MaryBeth asked no one in particular. "What about my being pushed into the elevator shaft?"

"Not the elevator incident, but, yes, I believe she had a hand in it," Butz answered. "For example, I think she was in cahoots with Treena Flowers to lure Sprat out of his apartment Sunday night and helped to delay his return. We'll have a heck of a time proving she was an accessory unless Ms. Flowers testifies against her. Even then, I don't know how credible that would be.

My guess is it would go the other way, first. Sadie testifying against Ms. Flowers."

"What do you mean? How might she have been involved?"

"Remember Sprat leaving the apartment door unlocked when he couldn't find his house keys?"

"Yes."

"Who spirited him away from the bodega to her apartment?"

"Sadie?"

"That distraction may have allowed Treena time and opportunity to stop by and assault her sister with the baseball bat while no one was there to defend an all-but-disabled Clover Sprat. Also, there may have been more than one blow to the same shin to insure Clover didn't wake up able to identify her assailant."

"Really?"

"Really. We didn't release that detail to the public."

"Can we prove it?"

"No, we can't prove that Sadie luring him away was part of a plot."

"Lieutenant," MaryBeth asked, her voice tempered with discouragement, "maybe you could charge Sprat with the death of Mrs. Swenson-Sprat, the wife before Clover. There's no statute of limitations on charging someone with murder, is there?"

"Mrs. Swenson-Sprat was fifty-seven years old, had a history of heart problems, died in 2007 and was cremated, in accordance with her own stated wishes." Butz swiped an open hand over his sprigs of hair and looked fatigued. "I'm afraid the opportunity—any evidence for making that case—is long gone."

"This is scary," MaryBeth said quietly.

"It's even worse than you think," Butz said. "Remember Mrs. Goodner at the rooming house told you Sprat turned up there in about 2006 as Howard Kluz?"

She nodded.

"There is no record of a Howard Kluz with that Social Security number before the year 2005."

MaryBeth studied him in disbelief. "You mean he may have been somebody else before 2005? Who?"

"Unless he tells us, we may never know." Butz drew a deep breath. "I could use a drink."

"Wheeler," MaryBeth said, suddenly turning her ire on her associate, "you should have told me there'd be days like this. You should have told me about the angst…the frustration…this feeling of helplessness."

He shrugged. "I could say it's because you didn't ask," he answered, retreating to avoid her advance. "The main thing is: You have to admit, honey, your career in detecting hasn't been dull."

Chapter Twenty
Done and Done

Gray and MaryBeth were silent as he drove them back to the office. Neither spoke to Ms. Yehle, who greeted them with her usual chatty enthusiasm, gesturing wildly as she reeled out reports of new dilemmas in the office.

Gray guided his gloomy protégée into his office where she dropped into one of the client chairs, jabbed an elbow into the arm rest, and propped her chin in her hand. She looked totally dejected. Gray leaned his backside against his desk trying to think of answers to the many questions he anticipated MaryBeth would be asking about justice denied and fairness ignored.

"Are we going to keep the check? Treena's seven thousand dollars?" she asked, breaking the silence.

"Yes," he said quietly, without looking at her.

"How can we keep it? Money she paid us to do an investigation that wound up getting her—our own client—arrested for murder?"

"Did we expend cab fare, dinner expenses, gasoline, picnic supplies in vain?" he asked, "Yesterday I promised you we would take every penny that came in the last four days of this month and pop it into the profit pot. No discounts, no rebates."

"Was that only yesterday?" She frowned. "I was impressed when you said those words, but it seemed much longer ago than only yesterday. I think I've changed since then, a normal person altered by all that's happened."

"It's called business." He smiled and shrugged. "If you sold tires and someone who bought your tires went out and got run over before he paid off the tires, would you worry about taking his estate's money for the tires?"

She frowned, not liking the analogy. "That doesn't make sense."

"Poor example, but you know what I mean."

She slumped against the back of the chair. "I suppose we do deserve reimbursement."

"Sure we do." He was eager to nail down his argument.

"But what kind of money is this?" she asked, backtracking. "Is this what they call 'blood money?'"

"It spends as good as any," he said. "Besides, now that she's been charged with murder, Treena Flowers will learn crime doesn't pay...very well, anyway...and we will have helped teach her that important lesson. Think of us as educators. You consider teaching a noble calling, don't you?"

"Did Lieutenant Butz tell you any of the details of how they plan to prosecute her?"

"He said the D.A. thought they had enough with Sprat's testimony to get by the preliminary hearing. Once she's bound over for trial, they're hoping the pressure will be enough to prompt her to plead guilty, maybe to some lesser charge. I don't know."

MaryBeth studied him a minute, and he braced himself for her next question.

"Wheeler, would you mind if I kissed you?"

Surprised, he recovered quickly. "Mouth or cheek?"

"Mouth."

"Yes." God, yes.

"You would mind? Okay, cheek, then."

"No, I meant... How much?"

"What?"

"Is this possible kiss worth a hundred to you? Or maybe a day's pay?"

"Money?" she gasped. "You think I would pay money to kiss you on the cheek?"

"It's the end of the month." He grinned. "We need the cash. Besides, it sounded like a seller's market, and we are a profit-making outfit these days."

Her expression became one of disbelief and annoyance as she stood.

Watching her carefully, he stood, too, and trailed her as she walked toward the door.

"Hey, MaryBeth...I was just funning you." His artificial laugh sounded hollow.

She whipped around to glare at him, nearly vibrating with indignation. He stopped his pursuit beyond her arm's reach, his joviality fading. He gave her a few moments before tapping his cheek with his index finger. "Kiss on the cheek? We'll consider it a freebie." He hoped his voice didn't sound as desperate as he felt. He was botching this, big time.

She crossed her arms. "Never mind. I'm out of the mood."

Wheeler's eyebrows arched in dismay, his tapping index finger slowing as MaryBeth turned and walked briskly through his open office door and out into the reception room.

"Denying yourself is only going to increase the want-to," he taunted in a Hail Mary pass.

"Hah!" she barked.

He darted past her and placed himself firmly between MaryBeth and the outer door, holding both hands up, palms toward his own face. She stopped and regarded him and his hands impatiently. Mrs. Yehle was nowhere to be seen.

"Do you find me attractive?" he asked.

Frowning, contemplating the question, MaryBeth re-crossed her arms. Reaching an annoying conclusion, she began tapping a foot. A moment later, she hissed, breathing between her teeth. He retreated a step. Her foot was the only part of her that moved.

"Okay," he ventured, "do you find me…proportionate?"

Her frown deepened. Her foot tapping accelerated.

Keeping a watchful eye on her face, he turned his open hands, his palms toward her. "What I'm asking is, taking into consideration my visible extremities, what have you imagined about the more intimate parts of me?"

Her eyes went wide for a moment before she rolled them. "Oh, for the love of—"

She shoved past him and swung the outer door of the office wide, almost hitting him with it. Sidestepping the door, he laughed out loud, then calmly shut the door behind her, turned back to his office with a smile, did a quick dance step around his desk and slid into his chair.

Tomorrow was going to be a great day.

He leaned back, propped his feet on his desk, locked his oversized hands behind his head and began to croon quietly: "She's got me…under her skin…"

A word about the author…

JACK SPRAT COULD is Sharon Thetford Ervin's thirteenth published novel.

A former newspaper reporter, Ervin has a degree in journalism from the University of Oklahoma, is married and the mother of four grown children. She lives in McAlester, Oklahoma, and is a probate clerk in her husband and older son's law office.

She is active in Romance Writers of America, Sisters in Crime, Alpha Phi Sorority, The OU Alumni Association, the Oklahoma Writers Federation, Inc., the Texas Writers Guild, the General Federation of Women's Clubs, and P.E.O.

Ervin can be contacted at www.sharonervin.com, on Facebook, Twitter, or by email at ervins@sbcglobal.net.

Thank you for purchasing
this publication of The Wild Rose Press, Inc.

If you enjoyed the story, we would appreciate your
letting others know by leaving a review.

For other wonderful stories,
please visit our on-line bookstore at
www.thewildrosepress.com.

For questions or more information
contact us at
info@thewildrosepress.com.

The Wild Rose Press, Inc.
www.thewildrosepress.com

Stay current with The Wild Rose Press, Inc.

Like us on Facebook

https://www.facebook.com/TheWildRosePress

And Follow us on Twitter
https://twitter.com/WildRosePress